Praise for Sharon Cullen's *Redemption*

"Sharon Cullen definitely has a talent for romantic suspense. ...Enjoy!"

~ *Ecataromance*

Rating: 5 Cups "I love the inviting cover of Redemption. Sharon Cullen immediately made me want to read the story of John and Hope. ...this well-written read that captured my heart. This extraordinary story has a too die for ending that made this reader's heart leap for joy."

~ *Cherokee, Coffee Time Romance*

Blue Ribbon Rating: 5 "REDEMPTION is an edge of your seat; thrill a minute, romantic suspense. ...Brimming with intrigue, mystery, steamy, yet tender love scenes and an adventurous plot, I found it impossible to put it down until I was finished reading it. REDEMPTION is one roller coaster ride of an adventure you won't want to miss!"

~ *Kimberly, Romance Junkies*

Look for these titles by
Sharon Cullen

Now Available:

Night Song

Love on the Edge Series
Deception (Book 1)
Redemption (Book 2)
Obsession (Book 3)

Redemption

Sharon Cullen

A Samhain Publishing, Ltd. publication.

Samhain Publishing, Ltd.
577 Mulberry Street, Suite 1520
Macon, GA 31201
www.samhainpublishing.com

Redemption

Print ISBN: 978-1-60504-340-1
Digital ISBN: 978-1-60504-217-6

Editing by Sarah Palmero
Cover by Scott Carpenter

First Samhain Publishing, Ltd. electronic publication: October 2008
First Samhain Publishing, Ltd. print publication: August 2009

Dedication

To my own redheaded hero, who's also named John. I love you.

Chapter One

The guy at the convenience store told her to take the old logger's road. Said it wasn't marked, but she couldn't miss it. That had been twenty minutes ago. She hadn't counted on the steep, winding hill, the sheer drop to nothing or the snow the weathermen were saying was a blizzard in the making.

Of course, she hadn't counted on being in Tennessee either.

Sweat made her hands slippery on the steering wheel and she tightened her grip. *Go to Callahan.* The urgently spoken words were a continuous loop in her head, pushing her in a desperate quest to locate the man named Callahan. Where was he? Shouldn't she have come across his cabin by now?

She leaned forward and narrowed her bleary eyes to peer through the windshield, but no amount of focusing helped her see through the white wall of blowing snow. The thought that she could have easily missed his cabin made her heart nearly stop beating and added to her growing terror.

The convenience store clerk had given her an odd look when Hope questioned her about Callahan. Maybe she shouldn't have asked. By asking, was she leaving a trail for them to follow? A hard wind rocked the car and she jerked the wheel to stay on the road. Her eyes began to water as the grief she'd been fighting tried to break through her weakening defenses. If she gave in to it now, she'd likely wreck the car. If she crashed...

No. She wouldn't think about that. She had to find Callahan. He'd help her. He had to.

Without warning, the road curved sharply. She yanked on the steering wheel and slammed on the brake. The car went into a skid. The rear end fishtailed, skating sideways. She screamed as the car sideswiped a tree, bounced off it, spun around and began sliding down a steep embankment she hadn't seen.

Throwing her hands over her face, she screamed again as the car turned end over end.

€

John Callahan stood on the dock and stared out at the pewter gray lake. The falling snow dusted his shoulders and snuck down the collar of his coat, but he wasn't quite ready to move on.

He needed to take one last look.

Say one last goodbye.

After a few moments, he shoved his gloveless hands into the ripped lining of his pockets, turned his back on the lake and walked away. His boots echoed hollowly on the wooden deck and he didn't look back when he entered the line of trees.

Countless times he'd walked this path. He'd even enjoyed the hushed solitude of the dense trees. But like everything else in his life, the enjoyment had vanished. Today marked a turning point. No more did he want to shoulder a burden that had become so heavy he could barely make it out of bed in the morning.

It was time.

He was almost to his cabin when a flash of metal made him stop. For a moment, he was too stunned to do anything but stare at the overturned car. Then he cursed. What were the chances of this happening today of all days? He didn't want to deal with this, but years of seeing to others' needs and the thought that someone might be seriously injured had him trudging forward, hands still deep in his pockets even though they were fisted in frustration.

When he reached the overturned car, he bent almost in half, swiped at the snow on the driver's side door and cupped his hands to peer in. Damn it, there was a body in there. He tugged on the handle. The door creaked and groaned as it slowly swung open.

Flexing and folding his fingers, he stared at the unconscious woman still seatbelted in. Clenching his teeth, he reached in and wiggled his hand in search of the seatbelt clasp. Sweat trickled down his temple as he groped for the latch and found the button. He hesitated. If he released the seatbelt, she'd fall. That meant he had to catch her.

Taking a deep breath for courage, he released the belt and shoved his arms out, grunting as he took the weight of her. She groaned. Damn woman wasn't even dressed for the weather. Where was her coat?

To get a better hold on her, he had to lay her on the ground. That crazy-colored white blonde hair of hers nearly blended with the snow and her head rolled to the side. Blood from her temple soaked into the ground reminding him of some macabre snow cone.

He hitched her up into his arms, ignoring the inner voice screaming at him to back away. Unfortunately for her, he was her only chance. Poor girl. As he trudged toward his cabin, kicked the door open and walked through the living room into the only bedroom, she remained unnaturally still. He placed her on the bed, then looked at her, hands on his hips.

So what now?

Get her warm, he supposed. The electricity had gone out with the start of the snowfall and he hadn't bothered with the generator, figuring he wouldn't be around anyway. He threw a blanket over her and made his way into the living room to start a fire.

Once the place began to warm, he checked on her again. Still unconscious but breathing easy. Pulse steady from what he could tell by looking at her neck. He threw another blanket on her, turned on his heel and headed back to the overturned car to search for clues.

There was nothing. No luggage. No purse. Nothing to indicate who the woman was, or where she came from. The plates were from Maryland. Why would someone from Maryland be in Tennessee driving the old logger's road in the middle of a winter storm?

Long-unused instincts stirred and he let out a frustrated growl when he realized his interest had been piqued. He didn't want to know, damn it. He stomped back into the cabin where a wave of heat hit him. Although he preferred to ignore her, he went to the bedroom where she still lay on her back, her head turned toward him.

The ugly gash on her head was beginning to crust over with dried blood and closer inspection confirmed what he had assumed from the beginning. A cut, nothing more. Might need some stitches, but probably not. He flicked off the double layer of blankets. She sure was a tiny little thing. Slim legs encased in dark denim. Tiny feet shod in expensive running shoes. If it weren't for nicely rounded breasts, he would have thought she was a child.

What in the hell was he supposed to do now? Even though it felt like a sauna in his tiny cabin, her lips were still blue. He had to get her wet clothes off and wasn't that something he didn't want to do? God, yes. The thought of touching her any more than he already had made his stomach roll, but it was either get her clothes off or have her die of hypothermia in his bed. It showed his state of mind when he actually had to weigh his decision.

This sucked.

He started with the shoes, because with shoes, he could pretend she wasn't a woman. However, when the socks came off to reveal pink-painted toenails, all pretense fled. Okay. The rest of the clothes had to go. He'd get the worst over with first. Wet denim was never fun to wear. But when he pulled up her heavy sweater, he snatched his hand away and stumbled back.

Holy crap, she was pregnant. By the looks of it, about five or six months. That bit of information took a while to process and get over. Did it change anything? Hell, yes. Now it was even more imperative to get her warm and dry. *Shit, shit, shit.*

Pulling off her jeans wasn't easy since the denim was wet and stuck to her clammy skin. Satiny underwear cradled her growing belly. Baby-girl pink underwear. She was into pink.

He ran a hand down his face and stared at the ceiling to gather his courage. Then, flicking a blanket over her bare legs, he started on her sweater by pulling out one arm. She whimpered when he touched the other arm. As gently as possible, he felt for broken bones. He didn't find any, but her elbow was beginning to swell.

Removing the sweater required putting his hand under her neck and lifting her head. Breathing deep, fighting inner demons, he paused. *You can do this.* Closing his mind to the smooth, cool skin, he pulled the wet sweater free and gently laid her back down.

Her bra was light pink with a little bow nestled between breasts spilling over the top. A blue and red bruise colored one side of her chin, but it was her stomach, rounded with child, that drew his gaze. He reached out, his hand hovering over her belly, then pulled back and fisted his fingers.

If he were any other man, he'd be wracking his brain to remember if he'd met the woman before and if the baby was his. He didn't have to think twice. You'd have to have sex to make a baby and he sure as hell would have remembered if he'd had sex in the last five months.

Goose bumps skittered across her skin and her hand moved to lie on her stomach. Jerked back to reality, John pulled the blankets over her, covering her from chin to toes. She sighed and snuggled into the nest he'd made.

He scooped up her clothes and, with one last look, walked out of the room, turned off the light and pulled the door partway closed behind him.

Outside the door, he absently stared at the wet clothes clutched in his hand. When he lifted his gaze, it fell on his weapon sitting in the middle of the kitchen table. Who would have guessed he'd be sidetracked by a mystery woman who'd crashed in his front yard and now lay unconscious in his bedroom? Pregnant no less. Just went to show what he'd known all along. Things never did go as planned. Especially with him.

In the laundry room, he draped her sweater over the dryer before searching the pockets of her jeans. He didn't find any identification, but he did find a fistful of cash. Ten one-hundred dollar bills.

No ID.

A beat-up car with Maryland plates.

Expensive running shoes.

The bedroom door creaked and he quickly stuffed the money in his pocket.

Eyes wide, blanket clutched protectively around her, pink-painted toes peeking from beneath, she stepped into the kitchen. They stared at each other for the longest time before she blew a stray lock of hair out of her eyes.

"You shouldn't be up yet." His voice sounded as creaky as the bedroom door.

She swayed until she leaned a shoulder against the doorjamb. "Where am I?"

Her gaze skipped around his kitchen before falling on the gun sitting in the middle of the table. What little color she'd had, drained as she took a step back.

John grabbed the Glock, released the magazine and put everything on top of the refrigerator, out of sight, hoping she didn't know about weapons and didn't realize there was still a round in the chamber. "You're in Tennessee."

"Tennessee?" Her surprised gaze slid back to his.

"Where were you headed?"

When she swayed again, he forced himself the few necessary steps to stand beside her, reaching for her elbow, not quite touching her, but ready in case she took a facer onto his hardwood floor.

"Maybe you should lie down."

"No." She stumbled back. "I, uh, need to go." Her brows crinkled. "Somewhere."

"Why don't you sit?"

When she was settled on the couch, haunted gaze glued on him, he sat in the deep leather recliner. "You thirsty?"

"No. Thank you."

"Hungry?"

She shook her head.

"What's your name?"

Delicate brows dipped. Lines formed on her smooth forehead as she stared at the pinewood floor. "Um..." Tiny teeth came out and bit into a full, pink bottom lip. Her breathing came fast, then faster. Blue eyes met his. Pale blue. Like aquamarines. "I can't remember my name."

Chapter Two

Automatically her hand went to her belly. It felt familiar, and in a world that suddenly didn't, she latched on to that as she frantically searched her strange surroundings, taking in the stone fireplace, the comfy couch beneath her, the warm blanket and cold pine wood floor at her feet. She was in a log cabin in Tennessee if the man with the gun was telling the truth.

Dark blue eyes—inscrutable eyes—stared at her. Red gold hair nearly glowed in the dim light. He was big. Tall. But then, at her measly height everyone was tall.

"Who are you?" she managed to ask through a throat quickly closing in panic.

"John Callahan."

Go to Callahan. The words startled her and she jumped.

His eyes narrowed. "You've heard of me?"

"Yes. No. I don't know." Oh God, she couldn't remember. "Should I have heard of you?"

"Don't know if you should or shouldn't, since I don't know why you're here." He paused a beat. "Or who you are."

She closed her eyes and cradled her aching elbow close to her stomach. Everything on her hurt. Thank God the baby was active or she'd be experiencing another terror. "What happened to me?"

"Your car overturned on the old logger's road."

"Overturned?" Her gaze went to the window behind him. To the snow blowing into drifts. "It's snowing."

"Been snowing for a good four hours. What were you thinking driving up this mountain in that?" His tone wasn't accusing, just curious.

What *had* she been thinking?

"You don't know your name, where you are or why you're here."

It wasn't a question but she shook her head anyway.

"I found this in your jeans." Hitching up one hip, he withdrew a roll of bills from his back pocket and slapped them on the coffee table in front of her. There must have been several hundred dollars there. "Do you always carry this much money?" His tone was hard. Cold. Different than the tone he'd been using.

Panic closed in fast and furious. What had happened? Who was she? The room became stifling. Far away she heard his voice, asking for her name. Name. Name. Name. She had a name. Everyone had a name. So what was it?

Callahan's face was suddenly in front of her. "...down. Bend down." He shoved her head between her knees. She took deep gulps of air and slowly the room stopped spinning. Or rather, the wooden floor she was staring at stopped spinning.

When she sat up, Callahan went back to his chair and crossed an ankle over a knee. Those dark blue eyes gave nothing away, no emotion, no indication of what he was thinking.

Go to Callahan.

She touched her temple where dried blood caked a large lump. "Where in Tennessee am I?"

"Smoky Mountains."

She stood and, on shaky legs, went to the window. There wasn't much to see besides lots of snow. "Why would I come to Tennessee?"

"I was hoping you could tell me that."

"I don't know. It's all—" she fluttered her hand in the air, "—like a blank slate."

"You're not from Tennessee?"

"I don't think so."

A long silence followed. It was quiet in his cabin. Almost too quiet. Her hand went to her belly as her chest constricted and a hollow feeling rose within her.

"Sit down before you fall over."

She made her way to the couch and sank into it with a sigh.

Callahan left the room. Cupboard doors slammed, silverware clattered. She rested her head against the cushion and closed her eyes. The cabin smelled of freshly sawed wood and warm fires. Something about the scents tickled something in her brain. A warm memory of other fires. A feeling of security. Happiness.

"Drink this."

A steaming mug was shoved beneath her nose. Instinctively she reared back and whatever memories that had been at the edge of her conscious vanished. "What is it?"

"It's not poison if that's what you're thinking."

She hadn't been thinking poison but his statement reminded her they were strangers and she shouldn't be so trusting.

"Look." He took a big drink. His Adam's apple dipped before he licked his lips and set the mug on the coffee table. "Nothing but tea laced with a little honey."

She took the mug, wrapping her hand around it and inhaling the sweet, warm scent. "Thanks."

"No problem." He sat in his chair again.

They didn't talk while she drank the tea. Callahan continued to watch her as she looked at anything but him.

Go to Callahan. Was it him? John Callahan? Was he the man she had to see? There couldn't be two John Callahans on this mountain, could there? Her luck, probably. So why was she sent to him? What did she need from him? Why...

Her mind became fuzzy and her eyes began to droop. Her limbs felt heavy and she struggled to sit up but soon lost the battle to fatigue.

John knew he wasn't going to get much sleep. Most nights he only logged a few hours before the nightmares stole his mind anyway, but tonight, with *her* in his bed, he damn sure wasn't getting any.

After she'd fallen asleep, he'd carried her to bed, gritting his teeth the entire way, and made sure she was warm before building up the fire and settling into his recliner to contemplate the flames and the bizarre turn his life had taken. Was she lying when she said she couldn't remember? He'd encountered enough people who lied without remorse to know that sometimes, no matter how hard you looked, you just couldn't see beneath the deception.

Some sort of amnesia wasn't all that uncommon in head injuries, but he wasn't a doctor, and didn't know if not remembering your own name was standard. But she'd been scared, wavering between trusting him and fearing him. Completely understandable considering she was a woman—a small woman—alone in a cabin in the mountains with a strange man. Yeah, he'd have been apprehensive in her shoes.

That led him back to square one, knowing nothing more than when he'd pulled her from her car. Except the color of her eyes. And the pitch of her voice. Gentle, soft, with an underlying hint of steel. He'd glimpsed a strong personality beneath her confusion. If only she knew—or would tell him—her name.

What he needed to do was call in the tag number of her car but the landline had gone down hours ago. Cellphone coverage was sporadic and only if he went outside. He wasn't stepping foot in that blizzard right now and chances were the call wouldn't connect anyway.

Even though he'd chosen to live far removed from civilization, he now cursed his solitude. If he'd built his house closer to town, he could call someone, take her to a hospital, get her out of his hair. He was angry because her presence made his home not his anymore. And the lonely mountaintop cabin had been his welcome respite for so long, it now felt violated by this pregnant stranger.

His eyes began to drift closed and he settled deeper into the chair. Part of him still suspected her motives and warned him to stay awake, but he honestly didn't think he'd wake to a steak knife at his throat. He was her only chance of survival in these mountains. Besides, if she killed him, so what? He had no problems with dying.

A scream jerked him from his sleep. Before he was fully awake, he'd grabbed his gun from the table next to him, was on his feet and racing toward the bedroom. A surge of adrenaline had his heart pounding in his ears as he burst through the bedroom door, weapon drawn, hazy mind trying to clear.

She was sitting against the headboard, the blanket clutched against her chest, eyes wide and unfocused. Her mouth was open but only small whimpers escaped.

After a quick glance around, he lowered the gun and advanced cautiously. “Hey,” he crooned, cursing that he didn’t know her name. “It’s okay. Just me. See?” He held his arms out to his sides.

She scooted back, making little sounds that reminded him of the small animals he’d freed from traps.

“Nothing to fear.” He tucked the gun in the small of his back and sat on the very edge of the bed, ready to spring if she lashed out.

Slowly her eyes focused although her body wouldn’t stop trembling. She was nearly buried beneath blankets, but it wasn’t the cold making her shiver. “S-sorry. Didn’t mean to wake you.”

“I was just dozing. Care to tell me about it?”

She bit her bottom lip, worrying it for a moment. “I-I don’t know. It was a nightmare.” Her laugh was shaky. “Obviously. I…” Her gaze went to the window. She seemed to look out the window a lot. “There was blood.” Her voice dropped to a whisper. “Lots of blood. I remember being scared…” Her voice trailed off as a lone tear traveled down her pale cheek.

“Tell me about the blood. Had someone cut themselves or was there more?”

“More than a cut.” She shuddered. “A lot more. I think… I think someone was k-killed.”

His stomach dropped. “What else do you remember?”

She shook her head, her eyes losing focus again. “Just the fear. Oh God, I was so scared.”

“Were you inside a building?”

She shook her head, then nodded. “Yes. A building.”

“House? Business?”

“I-I don’t know. House, I think. But it could have been an

office. There was a desk."

"Describe it."

Elegant fingers rubbed her uninjured temple and she closed her eyes. Then her fingers dropped and her eyes opened. Bleak, washed out, filled with exhaustion and fear. "It's all blurry."

He tamped down on his frustration. Had she killed someone? Was she taking him for a fool? Using him? She was such a tiny thing and when he looked into her eyes all he could see was despair, desperation and fear.

He stood and she lunged forward, holding the blanket to her chest with one hand and snagging his jeans with the other. Instantly he stepped to the side to break her hold and her hand fell to the bed.

"Don't leave."

He wanted nothing more than to get out of the room. No, more than that, he wanted her out of his life. To put her back in that car and watch her drive away. Because he didn't want to deal with whatever it was she'd just brought to his front door.

"I'm going into the next room so you can get back to sleep." Even he knew the stupidity of that statement. A veteran of more nightmares than he could count, he knew full well there would be no more sleep for her this night.

The blanket slipped, revealing a creamy shoulder and a pink bra strap. "Please," she whispered. "Don't leave me alone."

He squeezed his eyes closed for a moment. "I'm not fit company tonight. You'd probably be better off in here."

"Please," she said again, chipping away at his defenses. "You don't have to talk to me. I'll sit on the couch and be quiet." Her eyes begged. She was nearly on her knees in front of him in a pleading posture.

"Fine." He turned on his heel.

"Mr. Callahan?"

"What?"

"I need clothes. I can't walk around in a blanket."

That was the truth. The blanket was old, faded green and ragged, certainly not sexy until wrapped around her. He stomped to his dresser, pulled out sweatpants and an old sweatshirt, and tossed them on the bed, ignoring her outstretched hand. Once again he turned on his heel and walked out, breathing a sigh of relief when he closed the door behind him.

She probably needed help getting dressed, what with her injuries, but he was damned if he would be the one to help her. Undressing her had nearly undone him. Touching her again was out of the question.

When she emerged, she held the folded blanket in front of her. She'd had to roll up the sleeves of the sweatshirt several times and it still bagged around her wrists. Her slim hips, swollen belly and legs were swallowed whole by the gray sweatpants. Good, he didn't want any reminders of her pregnancy.

As she'd done several times that night, she peered out the window. He'd never bothered with curtains. No one came out this way, so there'd been no need for them, plus he liked the morning sun shining in. He liked being able to turn his head and see nature without the screen of gauzy curtains.

"It's still snowing," she said.

He grunted.

"How long do you think the storm will last?"

"Few days."

"Then we can leave?"

We? What was this “we” crap?

Staring at the fire soothed her. Just being in the room with John Callahan seemed to give her some solace, even though she knew he didn’t want her here. She got the feeling if he had his way and a storm wasn’t beating at his front door—and her car wasn’t on its top—he’d put her butt back in it and send her on her merry way.

Go to Callahan.

Her mind slipped back to her nightmare. Unlike the blood, she couldn’t actually picture the desk, but knew it was there. She rubbed her hands over her thighs as if to wipe blood off them. There had been fear. Terror. And shock.

“Do you…” She paused to lick her lips, the words sticking in her throat. “Do you think I did it?”

“Did what?”

“Do you think I killed the person in my dream?”

Another long pause. This one so long she finally looked at him. Navy blue eyes stared back. No emotion.

“I don’t know,” he finally said.

Her stomach felt like someone had hollowed it out. She’d been hoping for reassurances, but suspected Callahan didn’t do false reassurances. “I don’t feel like a killer.”

“What does a killer feel like?”

“I know I couldn’t take anyone’s life.”

“What if your life were threatened?”

Her hand went to her belly, to her baby moving fretfully. What if her life *was* threatened? Or her baby’s life? Her lack of an answer told her. And a deep instinct to protect her child told her as well. She’d do what it took.

"Do you think that's what happened? Do you think someone threatened me?"

He turned his gaze to the flames again. "You have bruises. Did you get them during the car crash or before?"

"You mean was I beat up?"

He grunted. He seemed to do that a lot.

All sorts of scenarios raced through her brain. Was the father of her baby an abuser? Had he beat her and that's why she'd run away? If so, where had all the blood come from? Maybe she'd been running from him. Maybe Callahan was the father of her baby and she was coming to him. For what? Child support?

As soon as the thought materialized, she wanted to laugh. Of course he wasn't the father. He could barely stand to be in her presence, let alone touch her.

"Instead of thinking worst-case scenarios, maybe we should try to figure out your name." He folded his hands across a flat abdomen covered in a well-lived-in and comfortable black and red plaid shirt. For the first time, she noticed scars running across the tops of his hands and distorting his fingers. When she lifted her gaze, it collided with his and for once, there was something there. A dare. He was daring her to say something.

"Ann," he said into the silence.

"What?"

"Is your name Ann?"

She scrunched her brow. "No. That doesn't seem right."

"Ann-Marie. Annabelle. Abby, Alice, Alicia."

"Are you going to go through the entire alphabet?"

"If we have to."

She folded her arm on the cushion and winced when her stiff elbow protested.

"You're hurting. What can you take? Ibuprofen?"

It was the first reference he'd made to her baby, and it would probably be the only one. It also reminded her that he'd undressed her. A reminder she didn't need. A pregnant woman wasn't the prettiest sight, but then what did she care what he thought of her body?

He pushed himself up from the chair and walked with a slight limp to the kitchen. Had he limped before? He opened and closed a cupboard door, ran water into a tumbler and shook out a few ibuprofen tablets. He limped back to her and placed the glass of water and medicine on the coffee table.

"Beth. Barbara. Billie." He sat in his chair.

"No. None of those."

"Cathy, Carrie, Caitlyn, Claire."

She popped the tablets in her mouth and took a drink, considering each name before shaking her head. "This could take forever, you know. And we may never stumble on the right one."

"I'm hoping one of them will trigger something."

What if she had a strange name or an unusual name? They'd never discover it. Her hands began to shake and she replaced the glass, more afraid than... Well, she couldn't be more afraid than she'd ever remembered, because she couldn't remember. She wanted to cry but figured Callahan wouldn't like tears.

She laid her head on the arm of the couch and curled her knees. She cupped one hand around her belly, finding comfort in the baby beneath. If she had nothing, she at least had her child. "I'm sorry."

He continued to stare into the fire. He seemed to prefer to do that than look at her. "What for?"

“For intruding on your life. I’m sure you have better things to do than deal with me.”

A sardonic grin twisted his mouth into a grimace. “Nothing that can’t wait.”

Chapter Three

Overly conscious of the woman sleeping on the couch, John quietly made his way into the kitchen. He'd tried ignoring her but that was like attempting to ignore an elephant standing in the middle of the room.

He pulled on his coat, hat and gloves and headed outside, hunching his shoulders against the stiff, frigid wind. Normally he kept a good stash of kindling on the back porch, but he hadn't expected to need any this morning because he hadn't expected to be here.

A large part of him cursed his dumb-luck fate as he trudged back to the house loaded with wood and tried to figure out what he was going to feed the woman. Food. Another thing he'd thought he wouldn't need.

When he got inside, stomping snow off his boots and brushing it off his shoulders, she was standing there, wrapped in her blanket, his sweats swallowing her up, eyes big, face pale.

He felt a sudden surge of protectiveness that surprised him. The last person she needed protecting her was a washed-up waste of a man who couldn't even control his own nightmares. "Not much to eat around here," he said as he bent to unlace his boots. "Wasn't expecting company."

"That's all right."

He hung his coat on the peg beside the door and placed his boots on the mat below. He'd never been a good conversationalist, and since moving to the mountains he'd become even worse. He could handle people in his job, but the art of everyday chitchat escaped him.

"I remembered something," she said.

"Yeah?" He paused in the act of pulling tea bags from the shelf and turned to look at her.

"There's this voice. It keeps going through my head. I think I was supposed to find you."

Rusty instincts kicked into gear as he placed the tea on the counter. "Why do you say that?"

"It keeps saying, 'Go to Callahan'."

Without realizing he'd moved, he was in front of her, crowding her, invading her personal space, his anger coming from nowhere and everywhere. "What sort of game are you playing, lady?"

What little color that had been in her cheeks drained. "I swear I'm telling the truth."

"Who sent you?"

She shrank back. "I-I don't know. I thought you might be able to tell me."

"How the hell would I know?" Names of his enemies scrolled through his brain, but the list was long and extensive, covering hundreds of cities and dozens of countries. "When did you figure this out?"

She licked her lips, and he could tell by the way her gaze flicked away he wouldn't like her answer. "From the start."

He drew back, shocked at her deception. "You've known from the beginning someone sent you here, yet you can't remember your own name?"

"No." She shook her head. "No. It's not like that. I really can't remember my name."

"You're lying."

"I'm *not* lying." She raised her chin. In a sign of strength, defiance or to mask the lies bubbling in her eyes?

"Tell me about this voice. Man or woman?"

"Man."

His eyes narrowed but she stared right back.

"Describe the voice."

She bit her bottom lip. Her teeth nibbled. Her tongue snaked out to lick. "I can't. It's like a whisper through my mind."

"Then how do you know it's male?"

"I just do."

"I swear to God, lady, if you're lying to me, you'll be sorry." A trite, clichéd threat, but one he would very seriously follow through with.

"I'm not lying."

He turned away, grabbed his coat and boots and stomped out onto the covered porch, slamming the door behind him. The driving wind almost bowled him over but he trudged through it, rounding the house and heading for her overturned car.

The implications of her appearance stunned him. For years he'd lived in relative solitude, having shed the physical bonds of his former life, but not the mental. Never the mental.

Go to Callahan. Why would someone send her to him?

She watched as Callahan hunched his shoulders and struggled through the wind. The sideways-slanting snow nearly blew him over, but he pushed through it. Just as she suspected he did with everything that came his way.

When he turned the corner, she gave up her post. A quick search through several drawers produced a pen and paper. She sat at the table and for a long time contemplated her lack of history. She closed her eyes and pictured the blood in her dream and the same word reverberated through her.

Murderer.

Go to Callahan.

Murderer.

The back door flew open and Callahan stumbled through on a burst of cold air and small swirls of snow. He stomped his feet and unbuttoned his coat with red, scarred hands. Once again he went through the ritual of hanging his coat on the peg and placing his boots on the mat below. Snow began melting in his reddish hair.

He pulled up short when he saw her sitting at the table, as if he hadn't expected her to still be there. His gaze cut to the pen and paper in front of her. "What are you doing?"

"I thought if I wrote down everything I knew, it might help me remember."

"Did it?"

"No. But maybe you can help."

"Me?" He raised an eyebrow.

"Sit and talk to me. Ask questions."

He studied the chair for a moment before sliding into it.

Noting she was right-handed, she prepared to write. "You said I crashed my car. What kind of car is it?"

"Toyota. An older model."

"What did you find when you searched it?"

"What makes you think I searched it?" His calm, shuttered

gaze met hers.

"It's what I would have done. Were there papers inside? Registration?"

"Nothing."

"Don't you think that's strange?"

"Very."

She bit her lower lip and stared at the blank paper before writing *Toyota, nothing inside*. When she looked up, something very close to humor glinted in his eyes. "What?"

"You always a take-charge kinda gal?"

"I don't know. I guess so."

He sobered and cleared his throat as if he didn't quite know what to do with his humor. "You were wearing jeans, a heavy sweater and running shoes. No coat. No boots. No gloves. There was no ID on you or in the car. And don't forget the thousand dollars."

She scribbled furiously then sat back and threw down the pencil. "That tells us exactly nothing."

"Right."

Their gazes locked. She could have sworn she saw sympathy in his and for a tiny second she wanted to lay her head on his strong shoulder, but she shook that impulse away before it could even take shape. "What's going to happen to me?"

"I don't know."

In a way she liked his direct, abrupt manner. It kept her from falling apart. "What if I never find out who I am?" Her hand went to her belly. How could she care for her baby if she had no name and no way to get a job?

"Hey." His voice centered her, eased the clawing fear. His expression had even softened, erasing the hard lines that had been etched around his mouth. “Surely you have relatives. Someone who’ll miss you. The phone line’s down, cellphone coverage is sporadic on the best of days, but let me try.”

The thought that maybe someone was out there looking for her made her feel better. “Who are you going to call?”

He hesitated and she half wondered if he’d call *America’s Most Wanted.*

“I know some people. They can tell me if there’s a BOLO out on you.”

“What’s a bolo?” It sounded deadly.

“Be on the lookout for.”

“You think I’m a criminal.”

“It’s used for missing persons as well as criminals.” He disappeared into the other room, returning with a slim cellphone and once again headed outside. She heard the merry chime of the phone as he turned it on, then the door shut behind him.

It didn’t escape her that he hadn’t exactly denied he thought she was a criminal.

Cellphone pressed to his ear, he stuck his finger in his other ear and tilted his head as he paced the small porch. His steps hitched as if his knee had buckled and he’d had to regain his balance. Then he was inside, shivering and shaking his head at the expectation that had to be on her face. Her heart plummeted. Foolish to think one phone call in the middle of a blizzard would solve all her problems.

He tinkered around the kitchen and came back to the table with a glass of orange juice for her, then sat back down. “Dawn, Delia, Desiree, Debbie.”

She shook her head.

“Ethel, Elaine, Ellen, Evelyn.”

"No."

"Maryland."

She glanced up at him. "What?"

"What about Maryland?" His laser blue eyes were intent.

"I've never heard of anyone named Maryland."

"As in the state. Did you come from Maryland?"

She cast her mind about and a puzzle piece slid into place. "I'm not sure, but I think so." She grinned. "How'd you know?"

"The tags on the car are from Maryland. When the phone starts working, I'll have a deputy run them. We'll see who they belong to."

Her grin faltered, then died. "You don't think they belong to me?"

"The car's beat up, definitely seen better days. You were wearing expensive running shoes, designer jeans and sweater, and..." His voice trailed off and he looked away. Swallowed.

"And what?"

A red flush crept up his wind-chapped cheeks as he stared at a point above her shoulder. "Uh, your—" he swept a hand in her direction, "—underwear is not what you'd call cheap."

She blinked. "Oh." Her face heated and she looked down at the table. Then the full implication of it hit her and she buried her head in her hands. "Oh, God. You know what this means?"

"It could mean several things."

She laughed and grabbed fistfuls of her hair, shaking her head. "No, it doesn't. It means we know one more thing about me."

"What's that?"

"I'm a thief."

"You could have borrowed the car. Or maybe you prefer to

spend your money on clothes."

"Maybe." Had she murdered someone then stolen a car to get away? *Go to Callahan.* Who the hell sent her here?

€

The rest of the day passed slowly. Too slowly. Callahan had no television and the radio was nothing but static. She spent inordinate amounts of time at the window, staring at a world of white. Worst storm to come this way in thirty years, Callahan told her. It didn't reassure her.

He threw a deck of worn cards on the seat cushion beside her and she played solitaire for a while, amazed at how many different versions she knew. How was it she could remember the rules to FreeCell but not her own name?

She ate not because she was hungry, but because her baby needed nourishment. At times she dozed but didn't allow herself to fall asleep completely, fearful of the nightmares that awaited her on the other side.

Callahan built a fire, fetched more wood, even took another walk. It seemed the walls were closing in on him too.

Just when the sun began to dip toward the horizon, his cellphone chirped. The unnatural sound had them staring at each other.

"Callahan." Even his answer was abrupt, just like the man. He listened for a few moments, walking around the room in an apparent attempt to get better reception. Cinnamon-colored eyebrows dipped low. A frown creased his face. Then his head shot up and he glared at her, his body going stiff.

"Right," he said into the phone. "Yeah, you're breaking up. I'll call you when I can." He flipped the phone closed and eyed her in a curious yet detached way. As if he were mentally pulling back from whatever he had learned.

"What?" she asked. "Tell me."

"How do you know Suzanne Carmichael?"

His eyes pinned her to the couch, twin gems of sapphire ice. As if sensing the sudden increase in her heart rate, the baby moved, stretched, then settled down. "I don't know a Suzanne Carmichael."

"Liar." He picked up his gun and her eyes went wide as he slid the top part back with a metallic sound.

"What are you doing?" For a moment, she pictured a bullet discharging from the barrel of the gun and ripping into her flesh. She shivered, trying to crawl farther into the corner of the couch. He stuffed the gun into his waistband. That was reassuring at least. He couldn't kill her with the gun tucked away. "What happened? What did you find out about me? Did I kill someone?"

"I guess so, cupcake." His tone was flippant, yet grim at the same time.

Her heart plummeted. She wasn't a killer. She refused to believe she would take a life. Not unless she or her baby were in danger. "Tell me about the phone call. Who was it?"

"A good friend of mine. Luke Barone." He paused as if to let that information sink in.

"And?"

"And, he called to inform me Suzanne Carmichael escaped from prison."

"And that affects me how?"

He huffed out a breath that would have been a laugh if it had come from anyone else. "Why don't you tell me?"

"I don't *know*."

"You don't seem to know a whole hell of a lot."

"It's the truth." How could she make him understand how frustrating, how disheartening it was not to know who you were? If there were people looking for you, missing you? If you were wanted by the police? She crawled up to her knees. "Please, I need your help. Something's not right. You have to believe me. I wouldn't kill anyone." Desperation lent urgency to her words and tears thickened her voice but she refused to let them fall.

"I'm not buying it."

"I don't know how to convince you."

His lips thinned into a narrow line while his jaw clenched. "Why don't you give up the pretense, cupcake. Come clean and we'll deal with it. Who are you? What's your name? How do you know Suzanne Carmichael?"

He'd apparently set his mind to the fact she supposedly knew this Suzanne Carmichael and nothing would change it, so she tried a different approach. "How do *you* know Suzanne Carmichael?"

His shoulders stiffened and suddenly he stood before her, so tall she had to tilt her head back to get a good look. She wished she hadn't when she glimpsed the raw fury, the tightly held restraint in the chiseled lines of his face. He leaned down until they were nose to nose. "That, cupcake, is none of your business."

He straightened, not the same man who had rescued her. That man had been aloof. This man was primed, ready for battle. The transformation stunned her and scared her too. This was a man she didn't want to anger. But apparently, she'd done just that.

"Tell me more. Tell me why I'm supposed to know this Suzanne Carmichael." Something tickled the edge of her mind.

Something about the woman's name. Then it came to her. Last year, Suzanne Carmichael's husband was running for president of the United States until allegations of oil price fixing surfaced. On the heels of that came the stunning news that Suzanne, while working for an anti-terrorist organization, had sold arms to a terrorist cell in South America.

"You believe in coincidences?" Callahan tilted his head and looked at her in curiosity.

"I guess. Sometimes." She eyed him warily.

"I don't. It's not a coincidence Suzanne Carmichael broke out of prison three days before you show up at my front door with a convenient case of amnesia and the mysterious voice in your head telling you to find me."

"You must have really ticked this woman off if you think she broke out of prison to find you. What'd you do to her?" She narrowed her eyes as another thought occurred to her. "Or maybe I should ask, what did she do to you?"

A muscle in his jaw flexed as his eyes turned flinty. "My past is not up for discussion."

"At least you have a past."

He shook his head. "You amaze me. You can quit the act."

"It's not an act."

"When is she supposed to arrive?"

"How would I know?"

"What did she tell you?"

"*Nothing.* I've never met the woman."

He pointed at her. "You're lying."

"Oh, yeah? How do I know you're who you say you are?" Her voice rose until she was yelling and she didn't care. He accused *her* of lying? You needed to know the truth in order to lie.

"*Me?* Who else would I be?"

"Maybe you're the father of this baby. Maybe I was running from you and you didn't like it."

The silence that followed was deafening. Callahan stared at her, his expression incredulous. She didn't need him to tell her how preposterous the idea was—it was written all over his face. Her cheeks heated in embarrassment and she shifted on the couch.

He turned on his heel and headed for the back door.

"Where are you going?"

"Out." His voice was tight, controlled.

"You're leaving?" Her voice rose to a squeak.

He didn't even glance over his shoulder as he stormed through the kitchen and out the door, grabbing his coat along the way.

Chapter Four

Her allegation hit him like a sucker punch to the stomach. It was ludicrous, of course. Absolutely ridiculous. He'd never seen her before in his life. She couldn't really believe he'd get her pregnant.

Her tear-streaked face, the absolute fear in her eyes—it worked on him. He wanted to soothe her fears, erase her nightmares. But that was the old John Callahan talking. The new Callahan was stronger, had learned from past mistakes. His body may be free, but his mind would never be.

"I've been trying to get a hold of you for days," Luke had said. "Heard about the blizzard."

John had sensed the caution in his friend's voice. That tone that said bad news was coming.

"Suzanne Carmichael escaped," Luke said.

Once upon a time, John had known terror firsthand. In that instant, he'd lived it all over again. He and Suzanne Carmichael had a history. She'd betrayed him, and he hated her for it. Now she'd escaped the supposed tight security of the federal penitentiary that had become her new home.

He'd been expecting it. Yet he couldn't figure out why Suzanne would want anything to do with him now, after all her dirty secrets had been revealed.

What was he supposed to do now? *If* Hope was linked to Suzanne—and all the evidence pointed to a connection regardless of his feelings—he couldn't let her walk free. A perimeter sweep around the cabin assured him all was safe. The snowstorm would keep people away for at least another day. He stood in front of her car, a barely discernable hump in the wintry landscape. Why would a pregnant woman deliberately harm herself and put her baby in danger to get to him? That seemed a little over and above rational thought.

Hell, nothing made sense anymore.

€

Light from the fire picked up the blond hints in his hair, making them glow. Some of the strands were still wet from his trek through the snow. He leaned against the doorjamb into the kitchen, sipping from a steaming mug, staring at her with a pensive expression. His shoulders flexed beneath the navy and forest green plaid shirt. The muted colors suited him. And why the heck was she thinking of his shirt and hair?

"I owe you an apology," he said.

"None necessary."

He shook his head, lips tilting in what she could have sworn was a smile. "Truth is..." He looked down at his hands and she stayed silent, watching him try to collect his thoughts. He seemed to struggle with it for some time. "I'm not very good with women."

She didn't know what to say to that. "No kidding," seemed a little harsh. Besides, she was touched that he'd reached out in this way, showing her a part of himself she was sure he didn't normally show people.

He cleared his throat. "So anyway, the bed is yours tonight. I think maybe we should both turn in."

And that was that, no further explanation, even though she was dying to ask questions, to learn more about this man who had so many layers she was just beginning to unravel them. And also beginning to understand that she would never get to the heart of John Callahan.

€

The dampness seeped into his weary bones. He would have been in pain if he felt pain anymore. Lately there'd been nothing but numbness. At first he'd embraced it. Now he feared it.

Reality returned a little at a time. That scared him too sometimes. When he'd first arrived, he'd managed to keep alert, barely dozing, taking ten-minute power naps here and there. Now it seemed he was asleep more than awake and that wasn't safe. Not here.

It was daylight. He could tell from the chinks in the cinderblock and the weak light filtering through the grates above him. Idly he wondered if it would rain today. He could use a washing off and a cool drink of fresh water. The thought floated through his brain, then disappeared like a puff of smoke. That happened often, the inability to concentrate on one thing for long.

Something sticky covered his hands. It was too dark to see and only a detached curiosity had him sniffing his fingers. He drew back at the coppery scent and frowned. Blood?

He tried to remember what had happened the day before but nothing came to him. All his days ran together. If it weren't for the grate in the ceiling, days and nights would be the same. That, and the beatings. The beatings always set his days apart.

But there hadn't been any beatings for a few days, so why did he have blood on his hands?

The sun began to slant through the grate, so bright he had to squint. He lifted his hands and stared at them as they dripped blood onto his pants and shirt. It was everywhere, not only on him, but splattered all over the walls and pooling on the floor.

Listlessly, his gaze followed the puddle to the river of red that flowed into it, until it landed on the crumpled, bloody form of a woman.

€

John lurched off the couch with a strangled gasp and kicked the afghan that had fallen on the floor. He stared at his hands in the dying light of the fire, turning them over, seeing in his mind the blood dripping on his pant leg. *Drip. Drip. Drip.*

Breathing fast, he wiped them on his pants legs, knowing in a deep part of his subconscious he was dreaming again. No, not dreaming. Reliving. And that was worse.

He stumbled to the kitchen, where he ran his hands under scalding water, watching his skin turn pink then fiery red in the same detached way he had in his dream.

Eventually his mind cleared. He yanked his burning hands back and wrapped them in a dishtowel as the nightmare began to fade. Reality slowly returned. The howling wind. The creak of his house as it stood against the elements. The hum of the refrigerator. His ragged breaths as he tried to regain control.

He fell into a kitchen chair, pressing his throbbing hands to his face, waiting for his mind to turn outward instead of inward. In the next room, his captive moaned, and like the caged animal he'd once been, his head snapped up, ears attuned. When he heard nothing more, he pushed away from the table and made his way to his bedroom where he stood in the doorway and watched her sleep.

A slim foot peeked out of the blanket, toes twitching. Her eyes rolled beneath her lids as her breath came in deep pants and her body tensed.

Shame hit him again. Shame at what he'd become. What he'd been. What he had done. Sickened with himself, he turned away.

€

While she waited for the water to heat, she rinsed out her underwear, then leaned over the marble counter, staring at herself in the mirror. Blue eyes stared back, somewhat familiar. An oval face. Pointed chin. Pale skin.

She turned away and paused at her reflection in the full-length mirror attached to the back of the door. She ran a hand over her belly, then turned to the side. A smile pulled at her lips as excitement bubbled inside her. A baby. It almost seemed surreal that in a few months she'd be a mother. A mother with no name. No past.

She stared at her left hand. No ring. Not even an indentation suggesting she'd worn one. When she looked back at the mirror, haunted, frightened eyes met hers. Who was the father? Was he looking for her? Desperate? Scared out of his mind as she sometimes was?

Steam fogged the mirror, distorting her reflection until she could no longer see herself. She shivered at the symbolism and stepped into the hot shower.

Callahan used the store brand of shampoo and soap, but it

got her clean and it smelled better than she'd probably smelled before. Even though it hurt the bump on her head and to raise her elbow, she washed her hair twice and stood under the hot spray for a long time, head tipped back, water pounding over her, easing the tension and aches and pains. But she couldn't ease the thoughts from her mind and eventually shut the water off and stepped out.

Callahan had big fluffy towels that wrapped around her twice. A quick search of his medicine cabinet revealed a brush. She ran it through her hair and used her finger to brush her teeth with his toothpaste.

She emerged from the bathroom feeling better than she had the day before and in clean sweats that Callahan had provided. The aroma of toast and coffee drifted through the closed door, making her stomach grumble. What she really craved was a tall glass of orange juice.

One was waiting for her when she entered the kitchen. Callahan was standing at the counter, pouring another mug of coffee and waved a hand toward the orange juice and a stack of toasted bread. "Sorry, that's all I've got."

"It's okay." She sat and reached for the juice. "If you knew the storm was brewing, why didn't you stock up?"

He paused from lowering himself into the chair in front of her and cast her a quick look. "Didn't have time. You remember anything?"

"No."

Elbows on the table, he stared at her over the rim of his mug. She noted the lines fanning from his eyes and the exhaustion just under the surface. She had slept well but apparently he had not.

"Francis, Frankie, Fiona."

Weary of the game, yet knowing it might be the only way to

remember, she thought about those names then shook her head and took a bite of toast.

"Gina, Ginny, Georgette."

"Georgette?"

He shrugged. "Watched a lot of Mary Tyler Moore in my day."

She laughed. It felt good in the face of all her fear. But it also shocked her. The Mary Tyler Moore comment indicated he had a sense of humor under the hard mask and that went a long way in easing her jumbled mix of emotions. It let her see the good guy beneath the gruff exterior.

He gave her a funny look. "I take it none of those ring a bell?"

"No." More at ease with him now than she had been before, she felt her shoulder muscles relax and the tension headache that had been near the surface recede.

He set down his mug and leaned back in the chair, tilting the front legs off the ground.

"You'll fall. Didn't your mother ever tell you that?"

"All the time." But he didn't lower his chair and she grinned.

She liked John Callahan.

"I believe you can't remember anything," he said.

"Last night you were sure I was lying."

"I've seen fear before. Your kind of fear can't be faked."

She tilted her head. He'd seen fear before? What an odd thing to say. "So what now?"

"Now we wait out the storm. It should blow over sometime this afternoon, early evening at the latest. Then we call in the tags on your car, find out who owns it and go from there."

"You still think Suzanne Carmichael sent me?"

"Nope." His chair came down with a plop. "I know it."

She shook her head and sighed. "It doesn't make sense. Why would she break out of prison, find me and send me all the way out here? Why wouldn't she come here herself?"

He turned his mug around in circles as he stared at it. "I haven't figured that part out yet."

She touched his fingers. Immediately he jerked his hand away. Maybe it was good she didn't have a memory because she sensed something in John Callahan's memory was bad. Really bad. Where had the scars come from? Why did he live way out here, secluded and alone? And why hadn't he stocked up on food before the blizzard of the century?

Maybe the weather had taken him off guard—after all, she'd been caught in the storm as well—but she didn't believe it. There was more to the story. And it wasn't good. She remembered other things, like the way he never handed her anything, but set it down for her to pick up. How, every time she'd reached for him, he'd side-step her.

When she looked up, he was staring at her, those blue eyes shuttered. But she knew that behind the mask lurked real pain.

John had lived with emptiness for so long that these new emotions nearly overwhelmed him. They came at him from all directions—fear, anger, grief, surprise. It was like coming up from anesthesia. Awakening from a long, complicated surgery to realize you were alive, you'd made it through, but it hurt like hell.

He'd come close to blurting out what had happened to him and it scared the hell out of him because he didn't know why. He'd never told anyone other than the doctors and even then he didn't tell the whole story. If the little lady was scared now, she would be terrified to learn of the monster that didn't live in her nightmare but was sitting next to her.

"I need to get some air," he said, the urge to flee so strong he almost tripped over her chair in his haste to rip open the kitchen door. He snagged his coat on his way and took a deep lungful of crisp, cold air. Hell, even that hurt. But it felt good.

The cold air dried the sweat that had beaded on his brow. The doctors had always said when the time was right, he'd talk about it. He'd been adamant the time would never be right and had vowed to take his memories to his grave. And two days ago he would have done just that if *she* hadn't shown up and wrecked his plans.

Breathing easier now, he watched a pair of deer emerge from the line of trees. The buck lifted his head and sniffed the air, muscles tensed to flee. The doe eyed John in curiosity. Behind him, the door opened and his guest stepped out, a blanket wrapped around her. He placed a finger to his lips, then pointed to the deer.

"Oh," she breathed. Together they watched as the doe snuffled through the snowdrifts and the buck stood guard, keeping a watchful eye on the two of them. John felt her hand slide into his and instinctively tried to pull away, but she held tight, curling her fingers around his. He glanced at their twined hands.

Her skin was soft, smooth, so pale next to his big, scarred hands. His heart beat fast as the panic closed in, but he pushed it away. Nothing would happen if he touched her. She was different. This wasn't Peru.

Closing his mind to the awful pictures in his head, he touched. He reveled. And for a long time they stood that way, hands held. But the memories refused to be ignored and the panic refused to be overlooked. Soon, old habits took over and he broke contact.

But for a moment in time, he'd felt normal. Almost...whole.

€

Their relationship seemed to change after the peaceful moment on the back porch watching the deer. She wouldn't say John was at ease with her, but...less on edge. He seemed to relax as much as she supposed he relaxed around anyone. And it didn't escape her notice that instead of thinking of him as just "Callahan", a man who could possibly help her, he had become "John", a man with a past and emotions like any other.

While they held hands, she'd experienced a connection she desperately needed. For nearly two days she'd felt isolated from the world at large, herself and human contact. John returned some of that to her, along with the realization she wasn't as alone as she'd been thinking. He may not want her here, but he was doing all he could to help her.

And true to his word, the blizzard stopped later that afternoon. The phone line would take some time to repair, he'd told her, and the cellphone kept dropping his calls. They spent another lazy day in the cabin, but this time she didn't feel as claustrophobic. This time she kept sliding glances at him hoping... Hoping what? He'd touch her again? He'd reveal a crack in his façade and show a little more emotion?

She stared out the windows, mainly because the scenery changed whereas the walls stayed the same. She liked to watch the blowing wind create snowdrifts, destroy them and build them back up somewhere else. Now that the wind had stopped, the sun peeked through weak clouds and the snow shimmered like a forest of diamonds, causing her to squint against the beautiful glare. Parts of her car were buried beneath inches of snow while in other places metal poked out of the landscape, marring what she considered picture-perfect scenery.

"You want to take a look?" John stood with hands shoved deep into his jeans pocket.

Unable to help herself, her gaze slid over the length of him. Over slim hips, long legs, wide shoulders. He was lean, but well muscled. An outdoorsman compared to a bodybuilder.

She'd never seen his red gold hair combed. Thick, with a touch of curl at the ends, it was always messy, leaving him with a sexy, just-out-of-bed look. His gaze met hers, navy eyes curious but aloof. He always seemed detached, holding himself at a distance. Was it her or was he that way with everyone?

She didn't know if it was disgust at herself for thinking of him in a way other than rescuer or sorrow that she couldn't penetrate the barriers he'd erected that made her turn back to the window. She had no business thinking of him in that way. After all, she could possibly be married.

"Let's go outside," he said. "No use brooding in here when it's beautiful out there."

She leaned against the rough pine-board wall, a half smile tugging at her lips. "That's the pot calling the kettle black."

"What's that supposed to mean?" No heat to his words, just idle curiosity. Did nothing get to this man?

"It means you're the king of brooding."

"Maybe I have reason to brood."

"And I don't?"

"Doesn't mean it's good for you. I should know, being the king and all."

She stared at him for a few moments, arms crossed over the swell of her belly. "Why are you being so nice to me?"

"You call this nice?" He waved a hand in the air. "Nah."

"Yes. I call this nice. At first you didn't want me here, did you?"

He looked away. "It wasn't the right time," he said.

"I'm sorry if I ruined any plans you'd made." With a storm brewing, she wondered what kind of plans he would have had. Unless the reason he hadn't stocked up on food was because he was leaving and had to stop to save her.

His jaw muscle ticked and he still wouldn't look at her. Then he shrugged again and pulled his hands from his pockets. "Let's take a look at that car of yours."

The day may have looked glorious from the inside, but once outside, the cold knocked the breath right out of her. John had given her an old coat of his and her running shoes. He'd been right, they weren't cheap shoes. She put them on, hoping once again for some flashback. When nothing happened, she fought the disappointment.

The snowdrifts sometimes came to her knees and she had to step high, falling behind John and using his boot prints as a guide. He dusted the car off with a gloved hand, slowly revealing an old black, rusted Corolla. The cold hinges screeched when he opened the door, echoing off the snow-laden trees and rending the air with a sound that violated the peace of the wintry day.

She crouched and looked inside the dim interior. Cracked faux-leather seats, blood on the steering wheel where she'd hit her head. But that was all there was. Nothing to indicate where she'd come from, why she'd ended up here. Disappointed once again, she straightened, rubbing her aching back.

John struggled to the back of the car and opened the trunk. A car jack fell into the snow, leaving a deep impression. "It's not a rental," he said. She didn't know how he knew that, but trusted his judgment.

The sun broke through the clouds again and she squinted against the glare.

She yanked on the steering wheel and slammed on the brake. The car went into a skid. The rear end fishtailed, skating sideways. She screamed as the car sideswiped a tree, bounced off it, spun around and began sliding down a steep embankment she hadn't seen.

Throwing her hands over her face, she screamed again as the car turned end over end.

When she focused, John was standing in front of her, with a worried expression. "What happened?"

"I remembered the crash."

"Anything else?"

She shook her head. Why would she remember something so stupid, something that didn't mean anything?

He must have sensed her frustration. "Don't worry. It's a good sign." He glanced around, his sharp eyes taking in everything and she wondered if he was looking for danger. It seemed strange that danger could inhabit such a peaceful place.

"I'm sorry if I led Suzanne Carmichael to you."

He swung back to her, his usually expressionless eyes holding surprise. As if he believed her but didn't want to. "Come on, we better get you inside where it's warm." He turned and she followed, but this time he walked beside her, leaving enough distance so their shoulders or arms couldn't accidentally brush but staying close. "Holly, Hanna, Hope."

She stumbled, fell to her knees and landed on her hands. Her breath whooshed out of her.

Blood. Blood was everywhere. All over the desk, turning white paper into a splattered mess. Her gaze flew around the room, looking, searching for...

She gasped, her hand flying to her mouth, and rushed forward. He lay on his back on the floor. When she crouched down and grabbed his hand, his eyes opened slowly, filled with pain and regret.

"Hope." He licked his lips and grimaced.

"Don't talk," she said. "Please—"

"Go to Callahan, Hope. He'll help you. He'll protect you."

Tears rolled down her cheeks, mixed with the blood staining his shirt and turning it pink. "No. I need to call—"

He squeezed her hand but the movement lacked strength. He'd always been such a big man, so full of life, humor, love. "Go to Callahan... His address...in the rolodex....take the card... Go, Hope. Don't let...them follow..."

He closed his eyes, his hand going slack in hers and she knew. She knew.

Slowly the snow seeped into her sweat pants, freezing her kneecaps. She stared at the snow, fully expecting to see blood. Tears raced from her eyes as they had in her vision, and an aching hole opened inside, quickly filling with grief. A soul-wrenching sadness that made her weak.

In the far reaches of her mind, she heard a voice. Someone crouched in front of her, the voice louder, insistent. Hands reached out, hesitated. She lifted her head, her vision blurred from the tears. She opened her mouth but no sound came out.

"You need to get inside," the voice said. "You'll freeze out here."

Callahan. John Callahan. The man she'd been searching for. Not to destroy but for protection. She struggled to stand, the snow beneath her giving way, making her stumble. A far-off noise registered in her mind and she realized she was crying.

"It's okay, sweetheart. It's okay."

She shook her head. It would never be okay. She didn't know what had happened, who the person was who had died holding her hand, but he'd meant something to her. Had been special.

They managed to stumble back to the house. Hot air hit her face when John opened the door, making her nauseated. She stood like a child while he stripped off her mittens, pulled off her coat and hat and scarf, then led her to the couch and the warmth of the fire.

He perched on the coffee table in front of her, elbows on his knees, blue eyes boring into hers. "Tell me what happened."

She focused through the pain, squeezing her hands together until her nails bit into her palms. "I'm Hope," she said.

He reared back. "What?"

"My name. It's Hope."

Chapter Five

"Hope." He had to chuckle at the absurd irony of her name, considering that was the one thing he no longer had in his life. Hope. "Tell me more," he said.

She huddled into the cushions of the couch and stared into the fire.

He wanted to give her comfort and cursed his inability to simply reach out. "Hope," he said out loud, hoping her name would pull her from the dark place she had gone to.

She turned her gaze to him but he could tell she didn't really see him.

"We need to get you dry and warm." He kept his voice gentle.

She shivered and hunched down. Her hair spread over her shoulders, catching the firelight and turning almost silver in the glow. "There was blood," she said, her voice detached. "So much blood."

Like his nightmare. The rivers of blood pooling around him. "How do you know your name's Hope?" He reached for the blanket thrown across the back of the couch and draped it over her shoulders.

"He said so."

"He?"

"The man. He called me Hope."

"Who is this man?"

"I don't know," she whispered. A small hand came up. Delicate fingers wiped tears from her cheeks. She sniffed and pulled the blanket around her. Again he thought of her wet clothes, how cold she must be. She needed to get dry and warm, but he could tell that until she was ready, she wasn't going to bother.

"Where were you when he called you Hope? What was he doing?"

"Dying. He was dying."

John wasn't surprised, had half expected her answer. No wonder her brain had turned itself off. "Who was he?"

Her bottom lip trembled. "Someone I loved."

Against his better judgment, he scooted from the table and onto the cushion beside her. He didn't touch her, but sat close enough he could feel her tremors. "I'm sorry." He ran a hand down his face. He couldn't deal with this. He had his own crap to deal with. Yet, he knew he'd never leave her to handle it by herself. Not now.

"He told me to find you," she said.

"What?" Whoever had died had sent her here? Not Suzanne?

"He said you'd help me. You'd protect me."

He surged off the couch, already shaking his head. He didn't want this. But the thought was distant and growing weaker. Something tugged at his heart. Compassion? When was the last time he'd cared?

After Peru, he'd walled off all emotion. For so many years he'd lived and worked, going through the motions but not caring. Deliberately remaining unconcerned, dispassionate. He could almost feel the sound structure of his internal walls groaning, creaking, threatening to topple with each drop of Hope's tears.

They came faster, her body heaving with the effort to cry, and he knew her own walls had already given way, leaving her vulnerable to a mass of emotions that could easily overwhelm and pull her under. Exactly what he didn't want for himself.

"Hold me," she whispered, staring at him with those huge aqua eyes.

"I can't—"

"Then hold my hand." She held out a hand to him. Her fingers trembled. "Please," she whispered.

He closed his eyes, the internal war inside him so strong it made him weak.

"Just my hand, John. I need you."

"You don't know what you're asking."

"I'm asking for comfort. I need to feel another person right now. To know I'm not alone."

Inside him, something cracked, the sound like the trees in the forest after a bad snowstorm, limbs unable to hold the weight any longer. He knew what it felt like to want human contact, the deep need to know someone was there. Before his mind could scream *no* he took her hand.

Hope closed her eyes. After a time, her breathing evened out and the tears dried on her cheeks. Her fingers still held his in a tight grip, so instead of pulling away for fear of waking her, John left his hand in hers and leaned his head against the couch cushion.

His hungry gaze roamed her face, thirsting for a look, starving for more of her touch. Light brown lashes brushed her cheeks, hiding the most beautiful eyes he'd ever seen. The flames of the fire highlighted her porcelain complexion and picked out the many different colors in her hair. Silver, touches of gold, strands of blond, all melded together and shimmered in the firelight.

He should try to call Barone again, yet he couldn't move. Didn't want to move. For once he wasn't panicking from the touch of a woman or feeling the fear that something horrible would happen if he touched too long, needed too much. And, oh how he needed. In a physical sense, yes. But it went deeper than that, far deeper. Into a soul that cried out at the solitude he'd forced on it for so many years.

Her fingers relaxed inside his and he knew he could pull away without waking her, but still he didn't move. He closed his eyes and opened his other senses. The smooth feel of her skin against his, the fire as it warmed him, the crackle of the logs, the comforting smell of burning wood. Hope's deep, even breathing.

The magic spell, forged by the comforting fire after the blizzard that had blown through his life, began to dissipate as reality slowly intruded. For all they knew she was married, her husband even now searching for her. The thought was like a knife to his gut, and he pulled his hand away, ignoring the hole that opened inside him. He leaned forward, placed his elbows on his knees and rubbed eyes that felt like sandpaper.

He left the couch, searched for his cellphone and went outside. There were no deer, just a setting sun bathing everything in a gloomy light. The temperature had dipped into the alarming range, but the winds had stopped blowing. To his surprise, the phone didn't drop this call and Kate answered on the third ring. After dodging pointed questions about when he was going to visit and how he'd spent Christmas, she finally put Luke on.

"What's up?" Luke asked.

"I need a favor." After the debacle two years ago in which Suzanne had tried to frame Kate for Luke's murder, then tried to murder Kate, Luke had taken over Suzanne's position as head of the once-secret, now not-so-secret, International Anti-Terrorist Task Force.

"Anything, partner, you know that," Luke said.

"I need to find out if there's a BOLO on a woman. First name Hope. From Maryland. Possibly the DC area of Maryland."

"Uh-huh." He could picture Luke taking notes as he spoke. "That's all? No last name? Age? Description?"

As if he could see her through the kitchen wall, John turned and looked at the closed door. "I'd say late twenties. Petite, blonde hair, blue eyes. Around five-five." Silver hair, aquamarine eyes, with a stubbornness and grit he'd never seen in a woman before. But he held those thoughts back because Luke would tell Kate and she would be at his cabin faster than Delta could carry her here.

"You thinking NCIC or local?" NCIC was the National Crime Information Center, a national data bank of fugitives and missing persons, among other things.

"Local." If Hope witnessed a murder, even if she were the murderer, the local department wouldn't put out a national manhunt for her. That kind of thing was reserved for the big guys—terrorists, cop killers and the like.

"Gotcha," Luke said. "You on your cell?"

"Yeah, but reception's sporadic. Still trying to dig out from the blizzard. Landline's down too, but I have a feeling I'll be moving out soon."

"Where to?"

"Maryland."

There was a long pause. John let the silence linger, unwilling to divulge more.

"What's up, Callahan?"

"Nothing. Just..." Just what? Helping out a friend? Stepping into something he should probably walk away from? "Just following through on something that happened down here."

"Where exactly are you headed?"

"Once you get me that information, I'll know. Oh, and I need you to run a plate for me." He recited the Corolla's license plate numbers from memory. Almost as an afterthought, he added, "And check on murders in the past week. Not gang related. At least I'm pretty sure its not gang related. White guy. That's all I know."

"Callahan, what the hell's going on?" Luke's voice was pitched low, probably so Kate wouldn't hear.

Something stirred inside him. Something he'd buried long ago in the hopes of never feeling again. Excitement. The thrill of a new mission. It was like a long-dead part of him was coming back to life. "Like I said, just following up on some things." The smile that spread across his face felt alien. Yet it felt good, too.

When he ended the call, he stared out at the landscape and mentally prepared himself to leave his mountain. Something he hadn't done voluntarily in a long, long time. And something he thought he'd never do again.

Back inside, he checked on Hope, then thawed some frozen steaks and made dinner. It was a good thing they were leaving soon. Food was running low and toast and steak weren't going to feed that baby of hers.

Thinking about the baby made all kinds of strange feelings

churn inside him. It was a constant reminder that she had a life to get back to, people who worried about her, loved her, missed her. The idea that he would return to his cabin after their trip to Maryland to be alone once again should have comforted him, but instead it left him sadly depressed.

He shook those thoughts away, condemning himself as the world's biggest idiot. He lived in the woods for a reason, steered clear of women for a reason. To think he could keep one small pregnant woman as his own was not only foolish, but possibly deadly.

You don't really believe that.

Yes. Yes, he did. Something inside him scoffed and that small sound left him shaking so hard he dropped into a kitchen chair to regain the strength in his legs. He stared at his scarred hands, a visual reminder of what he'd been through. One glance in the full-length mirror in his bathroom was proof enough why he needed to stay tucked away in his corner of the mountains.

"When you're ready to emerge, you'll emerge," one doctor had said.

"You'll kill yourself if you keep going this way," another had said.

Who had been right?

Two days ago, he'd thought it was doctor number two. Now he wasn't so sure.

€

Dinner was a series of sounds. Forks scraping against plates, ice tinkling in glasses. The hum of the refrigerator and the crackle of the logs in the next room. No conversation. No banter back and forth. For a man who ate all his meals alone, it nearly drove John crazy.

After dinner, they settled on the couch and the silence followed them, perching on the cushion between them. Hope seemed lost inside herself and John didn't know what to say to her.

"Do you know what it's like to grieve, yet not know who you're grieving for?" she finally asked.

"No."

She curled into what he now considered her corner with the blanket draped over her legs, her hands on her belly slowly rubbing circles. He watched her hands and wondered if she even realized what she was doing.

"I have no memories of the person who was killed, yet know I need to grieve for him. It's one hundred—one thousand—times worse not to know than to know and remember."

"I don't know about that. I have some memories I'd like to forget."

"I know."

"You do?" Her words startled him enough to pull his gaze from her hands to her eyes. They held a wealth of emotion, mostly things she was too young to feel. And he was too old to carry anymore.

"You're a sad man, John Callahan. I can see it in your eyes."

A sad man. He had to think about that since he'd never considered himself sad. People said he was gloomy, no fun to be around. Luke, and to some extent, Kate, tended to step lightly around him at times. But sad?

Hope stretched out a hand and he found himself reaching for it. It wasn't so hard, this touching thing. "We're a pair you and I," she said on a sigh. "One who remembers nothing and one who remembers too much."

€

The banging on his front door yanked John from the deepest sleep he'd had in years. He surged out of his chair and grabbed his gun.

Hope sat up, eyes wide, hair tousled.

John peered out of the front window as he plastered his back against the wall. When he saw his deputy's car, he breathed a sigh of relief and nodded to Hope before opening the door.

Bill Mercer stepped in, stomping the snow off his boots and brushing it off his shoulders. He clapped his gloved hands together and looked up, pausing when his gaze landed on a sleepy Hope. Shock flashed across the young deputy's face before he masked it and turned to John and nodded. "We were worried about you all alone up here." His gaze flickered to Hope again who had scooted to the edge of the couch. "I guess we shouldn't have been."

John grimaced, waved Mercer in and closed the door, shutting off the frigid air that had dropped the temperature in the room several degrees. He'd tried to get Hope to go to bed last night but she'd wanted nothing to do with it, adamantly insisting she'd rather sleep in front of the fire. So he'd settled into his chair, prepared to stay up all night and watch her sleep. Apparently he'd fallen asleep as well and he was well aware what the scene looked like to his deputy. For a man with a reputation for shunning women, this was one bit of information that wouldn't stay quiet for long.

Bill had his hat in his hand, twisting the brim around and looking between John and Hope, a thousand questions in his eyes.

"Everything okay?" John asked.

"Yeah. Real quiet. Everyone pretty much holed up for the storm." A smile broke across Bill's wide face. "My guess is there'll be plenty of babies born in nine—" His voice trailed off.

Ah, hell. Hope was standing. The blanket had fallen to the floor and it was very obvious as she turned to the side that she was pregnant.

Bill averted his gaze, cleared his throat. "Uh, well. The guys, they wanted me to come up. You know, to plow your road. That way if you needed to, uh, get out, you could. But I can see—" His face turned red and he looked at anything but Hope.

John was at a loss for words when Hope stepped forward and offered her hand. "Hi, I'm Hope. Mr. Callahan here—" she nodded toward John, "—saved my life."

Bill looked at him and he could feel his face heating. "Her car flipped over in my front yard right as the blizzard hit."

Understanding lit Bill's face. "Ohhhh. Sure." He glanced out the window. "Yeah, I can see the car now."

"Since I still have a few days of vacation left, I'm going to take Hope back to Maryland. See her home safe."

"Sure," Bill said, reaching for the doorknob. He nodded to Hope. "Nice to meet you, ma'am. I'll, uh, just clear that driveway so y'all can leave."

Hope rounded on him the minute Bill closed the door and stomped down the steps. "You're a cop."

"Yeah? So?"

"You didn't think that was something I should know?"

"Never thought it was relevant." He took his gun from the small of his back where he'd tucked it before opening the door and laid it on the table.

“Not relevant?” Her voice rose. “Of course it’s relevant.”

“How so?”

She waved her hands in the air, all up in arms about something he couldn’t even begin to imagine. Why should it matter whether he was a cop?

“It just is,” she finally said and he laughed. She appeared stunned, her mouth opening, then closing. “What’s so funny?”

“You are.”

She crossed her arms over her belly. “Why?”

It felt good to laugh. To really let loose a laugh that came from deep inside. He didn’t even bother to wonder how long it’d been since he’d laughed this way. Too long. And the situation wasn’t really all that funny.

“You can stop laughing now.” She tapped her bare toes on the rug. With her tousled hair, pink tingeing her cheeks and fire spitting from her eyes, she nearly knocked the breath right out of him. He did stop laughing, but only because he had this crazy urge to kiss her.

He took a quick step back. He could barely touch her. No way could he kiss her. Yet the thought was there, growing from an urge to a longing to a craving. He turned and walked away. “I’m taking a shower,” he mumbled.

Chapter Six

Hope fell onto the couch and ran her hands through her hair. So Callahan was a cop. She should have put the pieces together. The gun, the tough-guy image, the wariness. It all made sense now. Here she'd run straight to a cop. Had the dead man sent her here for that reason? How would a cop in Tennessee help her in Maryland? She rubbed her aching temples and closed her eyes.

Outside, Bill Mercer's Blazer plowed John's driveway while inside John turned on the shower. Hope flopped back on the couch and stared at the ceiling, refusing to think of him in the shower. Naked.

That was so wrong.

She could be married. She was certainly going to be a mother. She shouldn't think those things about a man she barely knew, even if a part of her felt like she'd known him all her life. And that wasn't so odd, was it? Because she couldn't remember her old life, just this new one. So really, she had known him all her life. All the life she could remember, at least.

The water splashed and this time she didn't fight the image of him standing under the spray, tilting his head back, long muscles in his back relaxing under the hot water. The sight of him laughing had nearly knocked her over. He had a deep, beautiful laugh.

She put her hands to her hot cheeks. "Geez, Hope. You're in trouble if you're thinking of him like that." No. No *if* about it. She *was* thinking of him like that, and that was bad news.

He emerged from the bedroom, his wet hair a dark red. He hadn't shaved and his whiskers were the same dark red, somewhere between mahogany and cinnamon. The man didn't own a new pair of jeans. All of them were worn, loose at the waist, frayed at the pockets and hems. He wore a dark gray T-shirt under a navy flannel shirt left untucked and unbuttoned.

"Shower's free," he said as he passed through the living room into the kitchen. She stood, but instead of going to the bathroom where it was probably still steamy from his shower and still smelled of his soap, she followed him.

"You told the deputy we were going to Maryland." She stopped in the doorway and watched him peer into the refrigerator.

He grunted in response.

"When were you going to tell me?" Part of her wanted to go. A major part. But there was a small part that wanted to stay here. That part felt like a little girl who liked to be safe in the place she knew instead of going into the big bad world where everything was alien.

He moved to the cupboards, opening and closing doors. "It's not some conspiracy." He turned and paused, apparently seeing something in her face that softened his expression. "You didn't think we'd stay here forever, did you?"

Maybe she had. Or maybe she'd wished.

"We need to find out who you are, Hope. I'm sure you have family looking for you."

"I know."

"I won't leave you until I know you're safe."

"Promise?"

"Absolutely."

"What about Suzanne Carmichael? If she's after you, going to Maryland wouldn't be the safest thing."

"I can take care of myself."

"You're putting yourself in danger for me."

His steady gaze held hers. "I think danger has already found me."

€

"Tell me about the woman." Manco Garcia's bottomless black eyes stared Suzanne Carmichael down. On the outside, he appeared calm, as if the dinner they were sharing was a cozy scene in a well-planned sexual seduction. Never mind they were in a sleazy hotel, eating fast-food burgers.

Suzanne tried to appear as nonchalant as Garcia as she took a bite of her hamburger and chewed. She wiped her mouth slowly with the paper napkin and schooled her features to stare at him as coolly as he was staring at her, while inside she shook so hard she feared her dinner would come back up. "She was as much a surprise to me as she was to you."

He gazed at her. The man never let his guard down, never entered a business deal unless it benefited him. And never let someone live who didn't follow through with their promises.

This last was what had Suzanne sweating.

He folded his hands over his taut belly. "This is a problem, Susanita. I don't like surprises. They...upset me. The woman, she witnessed something she shouldn't have. And she has what we need, no?" He tilted his head and Suzanne's fingers tightened, squeezing the stale bun.

She swallowed, her mouth going dry. Truth was, she didn't know if Hope Stewart had what they needed, but it would increase her life expectancy if she didn't let Garcia in on that bit of information. Damn, Bradley. And damn Charles Stewart. Both had kept her from the money she'd stashed from the arms she'd sold to Garcia and his terrorist organization, People of Light. She desperately needed the money now. Had promised a good portion of it to Garcia for his help in her prison escape. And if she were to flee the country, as had been her plan, she needed the cash to do it. Her cash. The cash Stewart had been bleeding from her.

"We have a deal, *querida*. Your freedom for two million of your American dollars." Garcia waved an elegant hand over the table. "I see you eating my food, enjoying my company. Yet, I have no—" he rubbed his fingers together, "—*dinero*. Certainly, Susanita, you see my dilemma?"

She cleared her throat. "I see you have every right to your...frustration."

Anger flared in his dark eyes but he quickly masked it. "Ah, Susanita, I am past frustration. It has been a week. I have met my end of the bargain. You have not."

"I will," she said quickly. "It's just a small wrinkle in the plan. You'll get your money, I promise."

A black eyebrow rose in disbelief.

She didn't really believe it either. Being Garcia's captive had not been in her plans but without the money, she couldn't leave him, and being a known fugitive she couldn't walk out of the hotel either. Which left her in quite a dilemma.

"Manco." She made her voice purr, the way he'd liked it all those years ago. "When have I ever not followed through with a promise?" She inched her chair closer to the small table and leaned forward, hoping the tantalizing view inside the deep V of her T-shirt would distract him. His hard gaze never left her face. "Hope will return to her father's home. And when she does, we'll get your money."

He stared at her until her face began to heat in shame and she pulled away, self-consciously tugging at the neck of her shirt. She hoped to God she was right and Hope returned to the scene of the crime. Garcia had placed two of his best men there to watch and wait, but so far it was as if Hope Stewart had vanished.

Garcia drilled his finger into the table. "I have been in your stinking country for two weeks now, called here by you. I can not afford to spend more of my precious time away from my business." A feral, angry Manco Garcia began to replace the suave man who had entered her motel room. Before her was the man who could whip his soldiers into a frenzy of murder and looting.

She hated this push-pull attraction she had for him. His dark side drew her while at the same time it frightened her. Right now she was frightened because she'd seen his wrath, saw what he could do to strong, brave men and had no doubt what he could do to a defenseless woman relying on his goodwill.

A goodwill that was slowly unraveling.

"We'll find your money, I swear."

His lips twisted in a sneer and he let loose a string of Spanish. Her fear rose another notch as his gaze locked with hers, hot and wild with anger. "Listen to me, *Señora* Carmichael. You think your prison cell with your running water and three warm meals a day was punishment?" He stood. He wasn't tall compared to American men, but he didn't need height to intimidate. "It is *nada* compared to what awaits you in my country. And do not think you can escape my punishment."

His gaze slid up her body, finally landing on the breasts she'd tried to distract him with earlier. A light came into his eyes and instead of the tight tug of desire she'd felt before, she shivered in dread.

"I have a very...specific punishment for you, Susanita." He leaned forward and brushed a knuckle over her cheek, then chuckled when she trembled. "You don't like my plan?" He waited until she shook her head. "Then pray Hope Stewart leads us to the money." He turned on his heel and slammed out of the motel room, jarring the plate-glass window next to the door.

Riveted to her seat, Suzanne stared at the closed door. For the thousandth time in four days, she cursed her decision to contact Manco Garcia even while she understood the desperation that had driven her to it. For two years, she'd sat behind those bars, dressed in baggy, gray prison clothes, obsessing over the money she and her late husband, Bradley, had secreted in overseas accounts. For two years, she'd devised and discarded plan after plan to escape, retrieve her money and disappear.

Bradley's unexpected death had caused a wrinkle in her plan. At least that's what she'd thought at the time. Now she was beginning to see it as a hurdle she may not be able to jump. Damn her husband for turning all the paperwork over to Charles Stewart and for giving him the key to all that money.

She mentally consigned Hope to hell for putting her in this position. The murder of Charles should have gone smoothly, especially with Manco's best men on the scene, but Hope had walked in, had seen the body, and Tomás and Ricardo had been forced to run before they could discover where Stewart had hidden her money.

Now Suzanne had no way to pay Garcia for her freedom and it seemed her time was running out. She'd escaped prison, but escaping Garcia's clutches was another thing entirely.

€

It took all of John's concentration to get them off the mountain in the nearly two feet of snow that had fallen over the past three days. Even so, he was acutely aware of the woman next to him. She'd changed back into her jeans and oversized sweater. Had twisted her hair into a braid that fell halfway down her back, which she liked to pull over her shoulder and play with the end of. She looked fresh and young.

His hands tightened on the steering wheel, not from the icy road conditions but from the emotions inside him. Had he known coming out of his shell would be this painful, he would have braved the storm days ago and dropped her off at the police station for Mercer or one of the other guys to deal with. Just his dumb luck he'd finally found a woman to pull him out of himself and she was pregnant, possibly married, with no memory and a killer on her tail.

He merged onto the interstate and picked up speed. Out here, the salt trucks had done their work, and the blizzard hadn't been as bad as in the higher elevations. Returning to civilization was always a tricky process for him. He far preferred the quiet of his mountain retreat to the noise and fast pace of the real world.

"What day is it?" Hope asked, running her hand down her braid and staring out the front windshield.

"Wednesday."

"Wednesday what? I don't even know the date."

"December twenty-eighth."

She shifted and he pulled his gaze from the road long

enough to glance at her surprised expression.

"That means I crashed on Christmas day."

He grunted his response, something he knew she hated, but did anyway. Doing things with the intent to irritate another person wasn't really like him, but with Hope, he enjoyed it.

"John."

"What?"

"I crashed at your house on Christmas day."

"I know that." He was well aware what day she'd entered his life.

"Why didn't you tell me?"

He blew out a breath. Not this again. She seemed to think he was purposely keeping information from her. "I guess I figured you knew that."

"I couldn't even remember my name, why would I know it was Christmas?"

He shrugged, still not getting why this was important. She seemed to fixate on the weirdest things.

"No wonder you were mad," she said after too short a silence.

"I wasn't mad."

"Sure you were. You didn't want me there."

True enough, but not for the reasons she thought.

"Geez, John. I ruined your Christmas."

"No, you didn't." That he could say with absolute certainty. She'd saved his Christmas. And possibly him.

"No wonder you had no food in your house. You were headed out for the holiday. Were you going to visit your family?"

He gritted his teeth, a headache forming behind his eyes. "No."

"Friends?"

"No."

From the corner of his eye, he could see her tilt her head. "Then how were you going to spend the day?"

"Alone."

"Don't you have family?"

He sighed. "Hope..."

"Humor me, John. Everything is a blank slate in my mind. I don't remember Christmases past. All I remember is blood and murder and this sadness that follows me. Tell me about your family. Let me live vicariously through you."

He understood. He'd been in her position before. She needed to connect to something. And while he didn't really want to do it, he told her about his family, leaving out that he hadn't seen them in years. That it had been his decision to sever all contact with them. That there were times he thought of them with deep grief and longing, but didn't know how to reach out.

"My mom and dad live in a retirement community in Arizona. My sister, her husband and their brood live in Michigan." Mary had been pregnant the last time he'd seen her. So that meant he had a niece or nephew he'd never seen. He knew his parents and sister were bewildered by his silence and his refusal to speak to them after his release. He couldn't explain except to say it'd been easier, less painful to pretend he was dead to them than to see their looks of horror when he'd returned, ravaged from his prison stay, the beatings and the illness that had almost taken his life.

His cellphone chirped and he snatched it, happy to end the conversation.

Hope pushed away her rising frustration. Every time she

got close to John, something happened to make him pull away. There was so much he kept hidden. Stuff she felt he needed to face. But she sensed the walls around his soul were high and erected years ago. Would she ever be able to breach them? Then she wondered why she wanted to. Dead bodies and missing memories were enough to keep her occupied. She certainly didn't need Callahan's problems as well.

So she concentrated on the passing landscape to see if anything rang a bell, prompted a memory or just looked familiar. While she knew they were in Tennessee heading for Maryland, and even knew the name of the highway, she recognized nothing. One good thing was that even though her memory stubbornly refused to reveal itself she was feeling better. Her elbow didn't hurt as much and her bruises were fading.

John ended his call and threw the phone on the seat between them. "That was Luke," he said.

"Yeah?" He'd told her he'd contacted his friend and Luke was searching the missing persons for her.

"You want the good news or the bad?"

"The bad."

"There're no missing persons out on a woman of your description with the first name of Hope."

Her hands tightened in her lap. As it always did when her heart rate accelerated, her baby began to move. "Maybe we were wrong about my name." She didn't think so. Hope felt right.

"No missing person of your description at all." He glanced over at her. "You are a true blonde, right?"

Her face heated and she stared out the window. "Yes."

"Thought so, but had to ask."

"What else? What about the car?" She didn't want to think

no one was looking for her. That she had no friends or family who missed her. What about a husband? Unless... She closed her eyes in despair. Unless the murdered man had been her husband.

"That's the good news," John said. "The car hasn't been reported as stolen. It belongs to a man named Daniel Webster. Sound familiar?"

Daniel Webster. She searched her mind. Came up blank. "No." Sudden tears blurred her vision.

"Hey," he said softly. "We'll figure this out. Promise."

She dashed the tears from her eyes with the back of her hand. "I can't believe no one's looking for me." Was she alone in the world? Just her and her baby? She sniffed, tired of the endless questions without answers. "Can't I just once get a break?"

"We have. I have an address for this Webster guy. He lives in Kingsbridge. We'll start there. Maybe you know him and borrowed his car."

"Or maybe I stole it and he just doesn't know it yet."

"Yeah. Maybe that too."

A few miles passed. Jon Bon Jovi segued into Madonna, then into Bob Seger.

"There's more," John said.

She rubbed her forehead and closed her eyes. "Can it get worse than this?"

"I don't know if this is good or bad."

"Just tell me."

"No one's reported a murder in the past two weeks. Not of a Caucasian male in a home or business in Maryland."

She flashed back to her vision of the man lying on the carpet telling her to go to John Callahan. Could she have made it up? Her mind playing tricks on her? "It happened. I know it did."

"I believe you."

"You do?" She looked over at him, desperate for his reassurance. It was all too much. No name, no family looking for her, a murder that either never happened or hadn't yet been discovered.

"I believe you," he repeated, staring straight ahead.

There was a sense of relief for her in his words. Whoever had sent her to John, had known what he was doing. John would help her. "Thank you," she whispered, leaning her head against the seat and closing her eyes. "Thank you."

Chapter Seven

John turned the engine off and they sat in the silence, staring at the house across the street.

"Look familiar?" he asked.

Hope shook her head.

"Let me go first." He reached under the seat for his gun and tucked it into the waistband of his jeans, zipping his coat over it. At the last minute, he'd grabbed the weapon, breaking all kinds of laws by bringing it across state lines concealed. He didn't care. Not when their lives could possibly be in danger.

"I want to go with you," Hope said.

"Hell no."

"Please, John. What if he's family? What if he's looking for me?"

"What if he's not? Hope, we have no idea what we're walking into here." For all they knew, Daniel Webster could be an abusive husband or lover. Maybe she'd even killed him in self-defense and that was the reason the car was never reported stolen. All very plausible scenarios. But none of them explained Suzanne Carmichael's role in this. "Let me get a feel for this guy first."

Webster lived in a bungalow-style house with icicle Christmas lights hanging from a wide front porch. The place needed superficial work like painting and new windows, but other than that, it was clean and well maintained. Next door, a tricycle sat on its side while one of those blow-up yard Santas waved at him.

As John stepped onto the sidewalk, a man stepped from the house and stood on the front porch staring at John's truck. He was a bit on the pudgy side, with gold wire-rimmed glasses and short brown hair. The man suddenly bounded down the steps and ran toward the car.

Hope stood next to the car, eyes wide, hand resting on her belly. John pivoted and ran toward her. His steps faltered as pain shot from his knee to his hip and he cursed the old injury. By sheer force of will, he reached Hope first and slipped in front of her. The man came to a stumbling halt, breathing hard.

"You Daniel Webster?"

"Yeah?" Webster's gaze flicked to Hope then back. "Who the hell are you?"

John felt Hope slide closer, her fingers curling around his.

"What's going on, Hope?" Webster took a step closer. John shifted his weight to the balls of his feet.

"You're Daniel Webster?" Hope asked, repeating John's question for lack of anything else to say.

Daniel's brows dipped in confusion. "Of course I am. You know that." He reached for her. She shied from his touch, taking a step closer to the only person she trusted in this mess. John's solid presence reassured her even though he stood silently, hands crossed in front of him, staring Daniel Webster down from behind dark sunglasses.

"What's going on, Hope? What happened? Why'd you leave and where've you been?"

She glanced at John, needing some sort of guidance, but he didn't even look at her, so she turned back to Daniel. "I'm sorry, but I don't remember you. I had this accident." She touched the side of her head where the bump was still a little tender. "I guess with your car."

"My God. Are you okay?" He took another step closer and Hope flinched.

"I'm fine. But I can't remember much. Just my name." She indicated John with a wave of her hand. "John saved me and found out the car I was driving belonged to you. That's how I found you."

Daniel gaped at her. "You only remember your name? You don't remember me?"

"I'm sorry. No. Could you tell me how I ended up with your car?"

He pushed his glasses up his nose. "Well, sure. Come on in the house. It's too cold to stand out here."

Hope shot a glance at John but he merely lifted his chin, silently telling her to for follow Daniel. She hated his stoicism, but understood why he was doing it. She'd sensed days ago that he didn't let anyone close, and now that they were finally going to discover who she was, he was distancing himself for when he would leave.

She experienced a flutter of panic at the thought of being without him. What if Daniel Webster was her husband? How could she live with a man she couldn't remember?

The inside of Daniel's house smelled of stale air. The furniture was old, worn, but well loved. Magazines cluttered the table and the floor next to the couch. Books were stacked haphazardly in various locations. A cat darted from under the scarred coffee table to cower beneath the couch.

Daniel cleared a spot on the couch and dumped the

mixture of books and magazines on the hearth. He kept shooting worried glances at John who stood by the front door and refused the invitation to come in any farther.

Once they were settled, Hope twisted her hands in her lap and cleared her throat. "Could you, uh, tell me my last name?"

Daniel stared at her for several moments. "You weren't kidding, were you? You really can't remember your name."

"Believe me, I wouldn't joke about something like this."

"This is so weird." He continued to peer at her through his glasses as if she were some specimen under a microscope. "Stewart. Your name's Hope Stewart."

She sat back, absorbing that information. Hope Stewart. Yes, it felt right. It fit. Not Hope Webster, but Hope Stewart. However, that didn't mean they weren't married. She could have kept her maiden name. She placed a hand under her belly, receiving comfort from her baby, before asking the big question. "Are we married?"

Daniel's eyes widened. He threw back his head and laughed. Hope shot a confused glance at John but he was looking at Daniel with an inscrutable expression.

"What's so funny?" she finally asked.

Daniel lifted his glasses and wiped his eyes. "Geez, Hope. You really know how to wound a man, you know?"

She leaned forward. "Please, just tell me."

Daniel sobered, a pained look crossing his face. "No. We're not married. Not for lack of trying on my part. We've been best friends for fifteen years, went through high school together. I can't believe you don't remember me."

He seemed hurt and Hope touched his knee. From the corner of her eye, she saw John stiffen. "I'm sorry. Please don't take it personally. I don't remember anything." *Except a possible murder*, but she kept that to herself. "Do I live around here?"

"You live in Essex." At her confused look, he explained. "Just outside Baltimore. You are—were—a school teacher."

"Were?"

Daniel looked away, a red flush creeping up his face. "You were fired."

She reared back. John shifted. "Fired?"

Daniel waved his hand in her direction. "The baby. You taught in a Catholic elementary school and when they discovered you were, uh, pregnant, they let you go. Something about not following the morality clause in your contract."

Her head began to spin and she grabbed onto the couch cushions. She'd been fired because she was pregnant? Nausea crawled up her throat and she had to swallow a few times. Suddenly a hand was on the back of her head and she was thrust forward.

"Breathe," John commanded.

Her dizziness passed and he let her up, glaring at her as if it were her fault her world was spinning out of control.

Daniel looked alarmed, his gaze jumping between John and her. She swiped some hair out of her eyes and took a deep breath as John stepped back to his post at the door.

"You need water or something?" Daniel asked.

She shook her head. "Tell me about the day I borrowed your car." She pushed the rest of her questions away to examine later.

"You showed up at my house late at night. Man, you were wild, almost hysterical, you know? You begged me for that Corolla I'd kept in the garage. Told me not to ask. Said it was better I didn't know."

"And you gave me the keys? Just like that? No questions?"

His expression softened. “Hope. I’d do anything for you. You know that.”

No, she didn’t, but she could sense it. Poor Daniel. He had a soft spot for her and she didn’t share it. “What day was this?”

“About midnight on Christmas Eve.”

“That’s all I said?”

He held his hands out to the side and shrugged. “That’s it. I’ve been worried sick. Tried calling your dad but he hasn’t been answering.”

“My dad?”

Daniel stared at her again as if trying to decide if she were joking. “Your father, Charles Stewart. Usually you spend Christmas with him.”

“Where does my dad live?”

“Bishop’s Gate. It’s not too far from here. ’Bout twenty minutes or so.”

She had a father who wasn’t looking for her, yet it appeared they were close. She wondered if John was thinking the same thing she was. And if he was, she wondered if his thoughts made him as sick as hers did. “I have one more question, Daniel. Then we’ll get out of your hair.”

“Sure. Anything.”

“Am I, um, married?”

Silence fell between the three of them. Hope could sense John’s tension, his nerves taut as he waited for Daniel’s answer. Hope looked at Daniel who had a tender look in his eyes, couched between sorrow and regret.

“No, Hope. You’re not married.”

€

John and Hope sat in his truck with the engine running, cold air blowing from the vents. Hope folded her arms over her chest and stared through the windshield. Her head was beginning to spin again, not because she was dizzy, but from all the information that had been dumped into her empty brain.

"What do you want to do now?" John asked.

"What do you think we should do?"

"That's your call."

She hated the bland tone of his voice, the distance he was trying to maintain. She didn't want distance. She wanted someone to hold her, someone she could lean on. She was so weary of trying to be strong. "Why are you doing this?" she snapped, turning so she rested her back against the door and could see him better.

"What am I doing?"

She waved her hand in his direction. "This. You're deliberately being cool. Acting as if you have no feelings."

"Maybe I don't have feelings."

"Bullshit."

For a moment she thought something close to humor passed across John's face, but he shrugged and the image disappeared. "Think what you want."

"*Stop this.*" She was nearly choking on her anger. Or was it fear? Fear that John would leave her to sort this mess out on her own. "Just stop it, okay?" Her tone lost its edge, replaced by weariness. "I hate this distance you're putting between us. You say we'll figure it all out but you won't talk to me." Tears clogged her throat and she tried hard to swallow them.

John put the car in gear and pulled out into the street. "I don't know what you're talking about," he said, his attention on the road as if something was going to jump out in front of the car and he needed all his concentration to keep from running it over.

"Yes you do. You're scared, John Callahan." She knew it was her fear talking. Stress, frustration, her emerging feelings for him and the fact she didn't want to think about everything she'd just learned.

He snorted in apparent disagreement.

"Yeah, you go ahead and think you have no feelings. Your problem is you have too many feelings and you don't know what to do with them, so you shove them behind that granite wall you've erected around your heart."

John stomped on the brakes and she braced her hand on the dashboard to keep from slamming into it.

"You have no idea what you're talking about," he said between clenched teeth.

"Because you won't tell me." She was nearly pleading now, needing some sort of connection to the only person she knew in this mess.

"It's none of your business."

She opened her mouth but he held his hand up to stop her, his tone softening. "No, Hope. It's none of your business. I promised I'd help you find out what's going on, but that doesn't give you access into my mind to pick apart my thoughts."

She slumped in her seat. He was so right. She was lashing out because it was easier to pick apart John's problems than her own. "I'm sorry."

He transferred his attention to the road and accelerated down the street. "It's all right."

"No, it's not. You're right. It's none of my business."

"Hope, you're scared. You learned more about yourself but

there's still so much more you don't know. I can understand that. I can help you with it. But I can't be there for you, not the way you want. It's not... I just don't have it in me."

John knew Hope felt abandoned by his withdrawal. He knew she wanted someone to lean on. He also knew he couldn't be that person. She was asking for things he couldn't give. Better to get that out in the open now before the little seed of hope he'd seen in her expression blossomed into something neither of them could handle.

Much better this way.

He refused to even consider his relief when Webster had said she wasn't married. Webster would be better for her. He obviously cared about her, didn't care who the father of her child was and would cherish her.

Ruthlessly, John stomped down on the sliver of jealousy trying to worm its way into his logical, realistic thoughts. *Practical* thoughts. She wasn't his. Never would be.

"He likes Reese's Peanut Butter Cups."

"What?" It took a moment for his brain to switch back to reality.

"Danny. He likes Reese's Peanut Butter Cups."

"He told you this?"

"It's something I remembered when we were leaving. And I call him Danny, not Daniel. He asked me out for our senior prom but I had a crush on Brian Alverson, so I said no."

"Did you remember anything else?"

She shook her head.

"He's a good friend." He should have left her at Webster's house. He would have taken care of her.

But there was Suzanne Carmichael to consider. In the

beginning, John had been convinced she had her hand in this. Then, as time passed, he hadn't been so sure. Now he knew for a fact Suzanne was involved.

When Webster dropped the name Charles Stewart, John's stomach had clenched. He knew of Charles. They'd never officially met, but he'd been one of Bradley Carmichael's advisors during Carmichael's ill-fated attempt at the presidency. From what John could remember, Stewart had been ambitious, yet solid, reining Carmichael in when needed. After Carmichael's downfall, then sudden death of a massive heart attack, John hadn't given Stewart a second thought.

This went beyond coincidence. Something was up and Suzanne Carmichael was behind it. That meant Hope's life could be in danger. And his too. Three days ago, he wouldn't have cared about himself. Now he needed to stay alive long enough to protect Hope and her baby from whatever was going on.

"I'd like to go to my father's house," she said into the silence.

"You sure?" Charles Stewart could definitely answer a lot of questions but John had a bad feeling about this. "We're both beat, Hope. Let's lay low for tonight and start over in the morning."

"I need to see him." Her voice cracked. She wouldn't look at him, but he'd bet money she was trying to fight her tears. "If it were your family, wouldn't you want to go back?"

The question was like a punch to the gut and he hissed in a breath. She couldn't imagine the pain she'd dredged up with those words. He'd severed the ties to his family so long ago he'd lost the way home. Unlike Hope, he couldn't go back.

Chapter Eight

The silence weighed heavily on Hope. She tried not to demand too much from John, tried not to be needy. She liked to think she was a strong person, but her edges were fraying. She needed to hold on to something before she flew apart.

"About fifteen years ago, this movie came out with Harrison Ford," she said over the low hum of the truck engine. "I always liked him." Funny the weird things her mind let her remember. "In this movie, he played a man shot during a robbery attempt. And when he woke up from a coma, he couldn't remember anything, not even his wife and little girl." She settled back in her seat, trying to find a comfortable spot for her aching back. "He even had to relearn how to talk and tie his shoes. I guess I should be thankful I can still talk."

John grunted, whether in agreement or not, she didn't know.

"But as he learned all these things, he also learned he hadn't been a very nice man or husband or father before he'd been shot."

John switched lanes and accelerated around a slow moving semi. The license plates said the truck was from California and she wondered if she'd ever been there or if she was one of those people who never made it out of their home state.

"Regarding Henry," John said.

She shot him a surprised look. "What?"

"The movie was called *Regarding Henry* and you're not like him. You weren't mean before this."

"How do you know?"

He shrugged, keeping his eyes on the road. "Daniel Webster. He seemed like a nice guy who wouldn't fall for someone shallow."

She supposed he could be right, but she still wondered. "I guess we'll find out soon enough."

As the last of the sunlight stretched toward the horizon, John turned onto a narrow, two-lane road bordered by barren snow-dotted fields.

"It used to be dirt," she said.

"What did?"

"The road. They paved it recently."

John took her new memory in stride while she refused to get excited about it. Who cared if the road was newly paved when she still couldn't remember what her father looked like or what had happened to land her in John's yard?

"Not many houses out here," he observed.

"Dad's house is the only one on this road. Except for an abandoned farm on down."

A few moments later they pulled into the driveway of an old farmhouse that looked as if it'd been lovingly restored. Hope studied it, at first with a detached eye. She'd had a cat once who loved to sleep in the boxwood at the corner of the house. In the summer, honeysuckle grew along the side, perfuming the air.

John turned off the car and they sat in silence except for the pinging of the engine and their mingled breathing. Hope climbed out of the cab and looked at the place she had called home her entire life. Her parents had liked the location because it was close to DC where her father worked, yet far enough away it was like growing up in the close-knit community of rural America.

She took a step forward and the edges of her vision blurred until nothing remained but the house, standing proud against the backdrop of leafless trees and farmland. Somewhere in the back of her mind, she heard John call her name, but she brushed it aside.

Four steps led up to a porch that spanned the length of the house. She stepped closer to the railing on the third step to keep it from squeaking. Her dad always said he was going to fix it, but never had. Then, when she'd gotten older, he'd refused, claiming he wanted to hear her come home at night and the creaking step was as good as a doorbell.

She smiled at the memory, hearing her father's words but not seeing his face.

Excitement churned in her stomach. No longer was she newly discovered Hope Stewart tentatively walking up the steps to face a father she couldn't remember. *She was Hope Stewart coming home to spend Christmas with her father, excited and apprehensive all at the same time, yet still angry and sad she'd lost her job. She loved her students. Loved teaching. And was angry the board had taken it away from her. Yes, she'd made a mistake. Yes, she'd gotten pregnant. But she was willing to accept the responsibility to raise this baby and continue teaching.*

They'd said since she wasn't married and wasn't going to get married, she'd breached the morality clause in her contract. "Besides, Ms. Stewart, how would it look to the parents and other teachers? You'd be an embarrassment to the school," one of the board members had said. She'd left the meeting shamefaced and hurt, but resolved in her decision to see the pregnancy through.

Enough of that. Today was Christmas Eve and she preferred to concentrate on what was to come instead of what had been. Her father, always supportive, told her to take her time, that she'd find another teaching job after the baby was born. In the meantime, he told her to live with him.

But that had been weeks ago. Since then he'd been evasive. Acting funny. He'd even told her if she wasn't up to it, to stay in Baltimore and they'd celebrate Christmas another day. As if. The two of them had celebrated Christmas together since her mom died twelve years ago. To leave her father alone on this holiday was unthinkable.

She opened the front door, noting he'd hung the fresh garland in the entryway, twisting it around the banister leading to the upstairs bedrooms, but he hadn't put the red bows on. At the first opportunity, she'd dig them out of the box of decorations stored in the basement. She shrugged off her backpack, heavy with presents, and let it fall to the floor inside the door.

"Dad, I'm home!"

The heavy sound of silence met her. She frowned. He'd known she was coming in tonight, had said he'd be waiting for her with a cup of hot chocolate. She put her suitcase down too and her purse slid with it. The house was cold and she rubbed her arms as she flipped on the light and made her way down the short hall that led to the back of the house. Somewhere, faint Christmas music played and she heard someone moving around in her father's den. Smiling, she turned the corner and headed in that direction.

Ever since the debacle with the Carmichaels two years ago, her father had given up the political scene and only took cases in the area. He was probably in his study looking over paperwork or reading one of his heavy law books.

She pushed open the door. "Hey, you. What're you doing working on Christmas E—"

Cheery Christmas carols played on the old radio in the corner of the empty room. No fire burned in the grate, waiting to warm her.

"Dad?" She heard a noise behind her, like someone was hurrying down the hall. She peeked out the door. "Dad? I'm home." Unease prickled her spine as goose bumps that had nothing to do with the chilly room popped up on her arm. "Dad?" She raised her voice, thinking, hoping he was in a different room. Upstairs maybe?

She turned to go find him when something caught her eye. Her father's shoes were sticking out from behind the desk. She approached, a sick feeling climbing into her throat as she followed the shoes to his legs. He lay behind the desk, his face waxy. Little gurgling sounds came from him as his chest labored up and down.

Blood was everywhere. All over the floor, turning the Oriental rug beneath him into a bizarre modernistic painting. His eyes opened slowly, filled with pain and regret. "Hope." He licked his lips and grimaced.

She knelt beside him, taking his hand in hers, as her gaze searched for the source of all the blood. "Don't talk," she said. "Please—" Had he fallen and hit his head? He was always in the best of health but maybe he'd gotten dizzy.

"Go to Callahan, Hope." His voice was thin, strangled. He'd always had a booming voice.

Her panic kicked up a notch. "What happened, Daddy?"

"He'll help you." He struggled to speak. "He'll protect you and the baby. Hurry."

She shook her head, tears falling down her cheeks, mixing with the blood staining his shirt. Obviously he'd hit his head and was confused. "I need to call—"

"Too late." He squeezed her hand but the movement lacked strength. He'd always been such a big man, so full of life, humor, love. "Go to Callahan... His address...in the rolodex... Take the card... Go, Hope. Don't let...them follow... Please."

He closed his eyes, his hand going slack in hers. A sob tore through her as she clutched at his arm. "Daddy?"

His eyes fluttered. "I love you, Hope." His chest rose, then fell. And then there was nothing.

"Daddy?" This couldn't be happening. They were supposed to drink hot chocolate. Decorate the house. Tomorrow morning they were going to open presents and attend morning mass. "No, no, no, no," she moaned, bringing his hand to her chest. "Please," she whispered to God, to her father, to anyone who would listen. He couldn't be gone. Not like this. He was all she had in this world. Her baby needed him. She needed him.

She stared at the blood covering his chest. Not his head. No head wound.

Go to Callahan.

Why would he send her away? Why would he be adamant she needed protection? He'd been struggling to tell her something. Something about people—"them"—following her.

A sound in the hallway had her spinning around. "Who's there?"

Silence except for the cheery sounds of sleigh bells coming from the radio. She swallowed the bile rising in her throat. The smell. Oh God, the smell of death. Of murder.

Go to Callahan.

Someone had killed her father. She stumbled to the telephone and lifted the receiver but there was no dial tone. The phone fell from her hand. In her panic, she knocked off the

Rolodex her father kept on the desk and it fell to the floor. Dropping to her knees, she picked it up, her hands shaking so hard she fumbled with the cards, pulling out several before she found one with Callahan, John *written on it and a Tennessee address printed in her father's block style of writing.*

Someone else was in the house. She could feel another presence.

Go to Callahan.

She swayed, her panic and the smell of blood making her gag, and hesitated in indecision. Which way to go? Then she heard another noise and she turned to run.

Instead, she slammed into a solid wall of muscle and screamed.

John clamped a hand over Hope's mouth as his other arm snaked around her back, anchoring her so they were chest to chest. She struggled, landing a blow to his shin that made him curse. Hooking her foot around his ankle, she yanked. Without losing his grip on her, he stumbled. His back hit the wall. She bit his finger.

"Hope," he said through gritted teeth.

She froze, her eyes going wide, but her body still taut.

"It's me." Slowly he removed his hand from her mouth.

She blinked until her eyes finally focused. Her body trembled and she sagged into him. "Oh God," she whispered. "Oh God."

"It's okay." For a moment, a tiny second, he struggled with the need to pull away, but she buried her head in his chest and the war within ended without a shot fired. He tightened his arms around her, hugging her soft, warm body close to his.

She'd scared the crap out of him when she'd entered that

fugue-like state. And he'd watched helplessly as she went through the motions of that night, knowing what was probably on the other end of it. He'd followed her into the house, watching, listening when she called out to her father in a cheerful voice and waiting for what was sure to come. What he knew had to come.

When it did, it was ten times—a hundred times—worse than he'd imagined. She'd crouched on the floor, holding a non-existent hand to her breast and it had set the hairs on the back of his neck on end. He'd wanted to pull her out of it but knew if they were to get to the bottom of this, she needed to relive it. It'd been a hell of a position to be in. His protective instincts screamed to get her out. To get them both out.

She wrapped her arms around his waist and even if he'd wanted to pull away, it would have been impossible because she held him so tight. For once, his panic and the need to withdraw stayed buried inside him.

"He's dead," she whispered, pulling away and wiping her eyes with the back of her hands. "My father's d-dead." She started to walk back the way she had come.

"Hope. Wait." John made a grab for her hand but she shook him free. He struggled to catch up with her, limping because his thigh hurt. "Hope." He grabbed her sleeve. "Tell me what happened."

She shook her head.

"I have to know, Hope."

Those aqua eyes were a deep blue, swimming in grief. Incomprehensible grief. She reminded him of a lost little girl. "I think he was murdered." Her voice was husky with unspoken emotions that skimmed the surface of her reserve.

He glanced through the door of the den, at the empty room. "There's nothing here."

"What?" Her knees gave out and she staggered. John grabbed for her, holding her as her breath caught in her throat. "He was there. I saw him. I talked to him. I—" she bit her bottom lip. "I held his hand as he d-died."

"When did you see all this?"

"Christmas Eve. In the evening. H-he was right there." She pointed to the spot where now there was nothing but bare wood.

He had a lot of unanswered questions and he wanted to go through the house, inspect each room, have Hope tell him if anything had been disturbed, but his gut was screaming at him to get out. He'd only ever ignored his gut once and that had cost him everything, no way was he willing to risk it again. He ushered her down the hall, but when they reached the front living room, she stopped and stepped close to the half-decorated Christmas tree, touching a dried pine bough.

Then she surprised him by scooping the stack of Christmas presents into her arms. Impatient to escape the eerie quiet of the house and an unseen enemy who he feared was nearer than they both thought, he took the gifts from her. Trying not to convey his urgency, he guided her toward his truck where they stashed the presents behind her seat.

As he pulled out of the gravel drive and accelerated down the road, headlights drew in far behind him and he stifled the urge to slam the steering wheel with his hand. He'd walked away from his life as an undercover operative when he was carried out of that prison cell in Peru, but when those headlights appeared behind him, every instinct he'd honed, everything he'd learned, kicked into gear and he became the man he'd turned away from long ago.

When he pulled onto the main road out of Bishop's Gate, the headlights followed, then dropped back but kept pace when he merged onto the highway and headed toward DC.

He changed lanes. It was nearly dark and he couldn't make out the model of the car behind him but he didn't have a hard time keeping track of the headlights. The right one was aimed just a tad off center.

He exited the highway and drove the side roads. The car kept its distance. An uneasy glance at Hope confirmed she was still in her mild state of shock. She was shivering and he turned up the heat, part of him glad she was in her own world and didn't know what was happening. He kept making odd turns, slowing down, then speeding up until he finally got his chance. The light in front of him turned yellow, then red. He stomped on the gas and sped through it. Cars honked, tires squealed and he gripped the steering wheel, hoping no one would sideswipe them. As he cleared the intersection, he glanced in the mirror as the other car rocked to a stop at the light.

Beside him, Hope leaned her head against the window and closed her eyes but was twisting her fingers in her lap. John wanted to reach over and disengage her fingers and hold them in his own. To offer some sort of comfort. Instead he kept his hands on the wheel.

In less than an hour, they were parking in front of Luke's place. Hope walked as if in a dream, her gaze straight ahead, her body rigid.

Once inside, John turned up the thermostat to warm the chilly townhouse. "Bedrooms are upstairs," he said, indicating the steps with a wave of his hand. "Kitchen's through the dining room."

Hope stood in the middle of the living room, staring at a blank wall.

"Hope?"

She blinked and turned to him but he knew, by the faraway

look in her eyes, she didn't see him.

"Sweetheart, you need to get to bed."

She blinked again. This time a tear formed in one eye. One single tear. Not a waterfall. Just a lone tear that seared his soul. He placed his hands on her shoulders and turned her toward the stairs, realizing this was the first time he'd been the one to initiate contact. The slumbering beast of panic stretched its muscles, a clear warning to stay away and he let go of her.

"Go to bed, Hope. Things will look better in the morning."

As if on autopilot, she climbed the steps.

"Luke and Kate's room is the first door on the right. I'll take the guest bedroom," he called after her. She didn't respond, and a few seconds later, he heard the door click closed.

He puttered around the house, checking locks and windows, peering outside. His connection to Hope's father was tenuous at best. They had a mutual acquaintance in Suzanne Carmichael. Whoever had followed them would have to know about that connection then link John to Lucas and he highly doubted that was possible.

Unless it had been Suzanne who had followed them. But as an escaped convict, how would she have found a car, then travel unnoticed when law-enforcement agencies all over the country were looking for her and her face was plastered all over the television?

Of course, the same thing had happened to Luke and Kate two years ago and that hadn't stopped them. He checked the street one last time and wondered if Suzanne had someone helping her.

There was nothing out there and he trusted his instincts enough to believe he and Hope were safe for the moment.

He rummaged through Luke's downstairs bathroom until

he found aspirin, shook a few out and swallowed them dry. Fire shot from his left knee to his hip and he rubbed at it.

The doctors had said he may always walk with a limp, but he'd proved them wrong. Now he only limped when he'd been sitting too long or did something stupid like sprint across the street to protect a woman from her best friend. He shook his head, feeling like ten kinds of a fool.

He followed Hope's path upstairs and stopped to listen outside the closed door. He hadn't heard the water run or any footsteps after she'd disappeared inside. He knocked and softly called her name. When he got no response, he turned the knob and carefully opened the door. She was sitting on the edge of the bed, her hands tucked beneath her, fully clothed. Tears had fallen but she wasn't crying now. He guessed she was too tired even for tears.

He rummaged in Luke's dresser, came out with a worn, oversized T-shirt and held it out to her. "Put this on and get into bed." Pulling her up by one hand, he shoved the shirt in the other. Funny how this touching thing got easier.

She took it and walked into the bathroom.

John stood by the bed, refusing to move until he knew for certain she was safely tucked in bed.

A few minutes later she came out, face washed, wearing nothing but the thin T-shirt and backlit by the bathroom light. The sight of her had him dragging in a strangled breath and reciting a prayer for strength. He closed his eyes and groaned quietly as long-dead feelings twitched to life.

With that white blonde hair highlighted by the light behind her and her long legs... He was only human. Even though he'd denied himself for so long, his body remembered. And right now it was on full alert and demanding attention, loudly screaming it'd been ignored long enough.

She stopped in front of him and looked at him with wide eyes. Her face, still damp from a washing, shimmered, and her hair fell past her shoulders. Her lips were full and rosy. He'd never noticed them before, how utterly beautiful and perfectly formed they were, with a slight pout on the bottom and a sexy bow in the top. He had a difficult time breathing, laboring to pull in one breath after another. His fingers twitched but he folded them into his palms.

He looked down at her rounded stomach. Right there was proof of what an idiot he was. Not only was she a woman and beyond his reach, but she was pregnant. And had just discovered her father was murdered. That thought had him taking a step back, but the spell woven around them didn't break as he'd hoped. He cleared his throat and turned to the bed, refusing to even contemplate what they could do in that king-sized monstrosity. He pulled down the comforter and blankets and fluffed the pillow then stepped aside.

Hope crawled in and he had to grit his teeth and look away from the sight of the T-shirt rising up, revealing a smooth, creamy thigh. She turned to her side, tucked her hands beneath her cheek and looked up at him. The absolute trust in her gaze brought him back to earth with a loud thud and he pulled the blankets over her.

"Thank you," she whispered.

A hunk of hair had fallen over her cheek and he ached to brush it away. But that was too personal. Too intimate. Man, he was so screwed up. "Go to sleep," he said gruffly and turned to leave.

"Don't go." Her voice was on that fine edge between fear and barely there control.

"Hope, I can't..." The thought of sleeping beside her had sweat popping out on his brow.

"Just sit with me until I fall asleep. Please."

The whispered please was his downfall. Who was he kidding? Hope Stewart was his downfall. He glanced around the room until he found a straight-back chair that belonged to a fussy desk. He grabbed it and positioned it beside the bed.

As she'd done the other night, Hope reached for his hand and only relaxed when he took it. She closed her eyes and after a few moments gave in to the exhaustion dogging her. Her hand relaxed inside his and with some relief, he pulled free, put the chair back and stood at the side of the bed staring down at her. His own fatigue had his eyes drooping, yet he knew he wouldn't sleep until he assured himself she was resting easy.

No dreams seemed to haunt her. Her chest rose and fell in an easy rhythm. Yet he couldn't leave without... Without what? He needed to do something. It was as if this force were keeping him there until he touched her one last time.

He could have touched her hand. That was safe. That was harmless. But he didn't. He pushed his boundaries, blocked the panic that reared up and leaned over, touching his lips to her forehead. For a moment, he closed his eyes and just felt her smooth skin against his lips, the warmth of her body and the clean scent of the soap he used and which she now smelled of. For a moment, he enjoyed the feel of touching another human being. Of touching a woman.

Until, inside him, the panic won and he had to pull away. But he took with him a gift. A gift he would take out and cherish when the dark winter nights in his lonesome cabin got to be too much. When he wanted to remember what could have been, instead of what was.

Chapter Nine

Sleep wasn't going to come to him this night. He didn't even try. Instead, John went downstairs and flipped on the gas fireplace, scowling at the modern convenience. He was a firm believer in splitting your own logs, the reward being the smell and comfort of a crackling fire. He settled into a leather chair and stared at the flames, turning what little he knew over in his head.

A man killed, yet no body. A prison escapee who had a link to the missing dead man. No evidence of foul play. No sign of foul deeds. A woman with a faulty memory.

Absently rubbing his aching thigh, he once again tried to put the pieces together. But instead his brain chose to think of the fire shooting from Hope's eyes as they left Daniel Webster's house. Damn but that spurt of life inside her had done something to him. Didn't matter that he was the target of her anger, he'd been fascinated. Until he listened to what she was saying.

Hell, he knew he was scared. No big secret there. But when she oh-so kindly told him what he was scared of, he'd about run off the road. His feelings? Impossible. He didn't have any feelings. Hadn't felt anything worthwhile since Peru. So to be afraid of something he didn't even feel—well, that was just ridiculous.

Your problem is you have too many feelings and you don't know what to do with them, so you shove them behind that granite wall you've erected around your heart.

That granite wall gave a loud crack, bits and pieces of it falling away, revealing what lay beneath. No, Hope Stewart had been wrong. There was no heart behind that wall. Nothing but a black hole where a heart once beat strong and sure. Before Peru. Before Angelina.

Suddenly restless, he stood, needing to do something to keep his mind occupied and away from things that would haunt him. He snapped off the fake fireplace and trudged up the steps. His leg only whimpered a time or two, the aspirin having done its job. As he passed Hope's room, he paused and placed his fingers against the door. When he peeked in, she was curled in a ball, asleep.

Sometimes sleep was the best thing, unless of course the demons you were trying to escape invaded your dreams. Then sleep could become a prison, trapping you in your nightmares, forcing you to relive things you'd just as soon forget. He walked on, entered the guest room, and while he wrestled with his decision not to call the police, once again checked the streets for any sign of the car that had followed them.

What would he have told the cops if he'd called? Hope's father had been killed but they couldn't find the body? She'd witnessed the murder but fled the scene without calling the police? She'd disappeared for three days, claiming to have lost her memory?

His actions on autopilot, he stripped off his clothes and climbed into bed in his boxers. He stared at the ceiling as he lay on his back, hands behind his head. Outside, a car cruised past but traveled on. Inside, the furnace kicked on and somewhere in the room a clock ticked by the seconds. He wondered if Hope was sleeping soundly. If, even in sleep, she grieved.

Hope.

Funny thing about life was you never knew what was coming next. One day you're boarding a plane to Peru to kick some terrorist ass, the next you're imprisoned, tortured, near death. One day you're saying your final goodbyes to a life that had turned on you, the next you're caring for a woman who crashed into your yard bringing...hope.

Yeah, funny how things could change in the blink of an eye. He bet Hope never imagined her life would irrevocably change as she walked into her father's home for Christmas. Probably never imagined running for her life to a man who'd given up on life.

Irony didn't even begin to describe it.

His lids drooped, and as he drifted off to sleep, *chocolate-colored eyes looked into his. Serious, yet with a spark of humor. Rich, dark hair surrounded a round face. There were crinkles in the corners of her eyes, indicating that at one time she used to laugh often.*

Angelina. Her name meant angel. And she was that. At least to him. His angel surrounded by hell. "¿Como esta?" she whispered in her native tongue.

He scooted to a sitting position, trying to hide his wince of pain. "Bien." It was their ritual. She would ask how he was, he would reply in the positive even though they both knew he was full of shit.

Little did she know—or maybe she did know—that his day revolved around her visits. He would eagerly await the rancid meals she served him. And she seemed to enjoy their too-brief visits as well.

Setting the dented tray at his feet, she threw a worried glance over her shoulder before touching his uninjured leg. He closed his eyes at the feel of a healing touch, a touch that didn't bring pain and humiliation. "¿Te hizo daño?" Did he hurt you?

"No." They both knew it was a lie, just as they both knew there wasn't a damn thing she could do about his injuries except give what comfort she could.

Concern shadowed her dark eyes. He was already half in love with her even though they spent mere minutes a day in each other's presence.

"Ah, mi soldado valiente." She cupped his cheek. Her skin was soft and warm and smelled of the food she'd been cooking.

Brave soldier? He didn't think so. He was anything but brave, breaking under the terrorists' interrogation tactics, screaming when the pain became intolerable. No, he was anything but brave. But if she wanted to believe that, he'd let her. He turned his face into her palm and kissed her hand.

She pulled away in surprise, cradling her hand close to her breast. Tears filled her eyes. "Gracias."

Ah, but he should be the one thanking her. For just a few minutes each day, she made him feel human, made him forget the pain, the humiliation, the terror. "No, Angelina, thank you." He waved his hand in the air, motioning her toward the door. He didn't want her to go, but his fear of being caught in something as innocent as a small conversation overrode his own desires. "Go, por favor."

Her smile faltered, then died. He hated to see it vanish, like the sun setting on another day, not knowing if you were going to be here to see the next one. When he was alone in his cell, staring at the mold-covered cinderblock walls, he envisioned breaking out of this hellhole, snatching his Angelina and carrying her to America. He'd build her a home. A nice cabin on a lake where they could live without fear. He would erase the shadows in her eyes and she would heal the soul the terrorists had ripped apart.

That was his dream. A dream based on a few minutes of conversation once a day. Yet he knew that deep inside of them, there was a connection. Angelina felt for him as he felt for her.

He listened to her soft footsteps as she walked away, heard the laughter of the guards, her squeal of surprise. He surged up. His broken leg crumpled beneath him and, with a cry of pain, he stumbled and slammed his dislocated shoulder into the cement wall.

"Angelina!" He cried out her name before he could stop himself, then cursed his stupidity. The guards probably heard and they would retaliate.

Angelina screamed, the sound echoing off the walls, resounding in his heart and shattering it like fragile glass. He lurched toward the door, pressed his forehead against the heavy bars to see what was happening. There was a scuffle, more laughter. Evil laughter.

"Angelina!" He screamed her name this time, his blood pounding in his ears, hands fisting the rough metal of the bars.

Nothing but silence bounced back at him.

€

Garcia charged into the room, a swirling presence of hot Latino and angry terrorist. Suzanne didn't know whether to be relieved he'd returned or frightened. She hadn't heard from him all day, had been left to her own devices in the seemingly abandoned ratty motel room.

She'd thought about escaping, had even gone so far as to open the door of the room and look out. But the presence of one of Garcia's men outside and the fact that, at this point, Garcia was her only chance at survival, changed her mind.

"The woman is back," he said, cutting the air with a slice of his hand.

"What woman?"

Irritation crossed his face. "Stewart's daughter. Tomás has been—how do you call it? Staking out her father's *casa* ever since she disappeared. She returned early this evening." His nearly black eyes narrowed on her. "She had a man with her."

A shiver rippled up Suzanne's spine and she fought hard not to let Garcia see it. This didn't bode well for her. They needed Hope Stewart. More specifically, they needed what she had. A man in the picture was not good. The only thing worse would be the police.

"Who is this man, Susanita?"

"What did he look like?"

He placed his hands on slim hips. As always, he was impeccably dressed in all black. And as always, the effect was devastating and dangerous. He was ruthless, brutal and cold-blooded, all the reasons she'd cited when she'd contacted him to help her. If she had only known how screwed up this was going to get, she would have stayed in prison.

A black eyebrow rose as he stared at her with bottomless eyes. "It was dark. Tómas could not see the man well. They were in the house less than an hour. Tómas tried to follow but lost them."

This was not good.

"Who could she have run to, Susanita?"

"I don't know."

He took a threatening step toward her, his eyes flashing. "You play games with me, *puta*?"

She stood from the bed, anger making her foolish. "I am not

a whore."

Garcia loomed over her, the rich scent of his cologne surrounding her, strangling her other senses. "No? Then what are you?" He stroked her cheek with the back of his knuckles. Something glittered in his eyes and she refused to acknowledge what. "You ask me for a favor and promise me money, yet I see no money."

He straightened and she fought the urge to close her eyes in relief. Her heart nearly beat through her chest and her strangled breaths came too fast.

"If I don't get my money, you will become my *puta*, yes?"

She swallowed, her throat so dry it hurt. "No," she whispered.

His smile was anything but reassuring. "You will, *mi Susanita*. You will. Now tell me, who is this man Hope Stewart runs to?"

"I don't know. Honestly, Manco, I have no idea."

The blow to her face snapped her head back. Stars danced before her eyes and she stumbled backward, falling on the bed. She reached up and touched her bleeding cheek.

Garcia watched her, hands in his pockets, as if nothing had happened but a friendly conversation between two acquaintances. She'd been afraid of him a few times since he'd released her from prison, but her fear doubled and she began to wonder, when she finally found her money, would it be enough?

He shrugged elegantly clad shoulders. "Think of it as a warning, *mi amor*. If I don't get my money, it will be far worse." He turned and sauntered to the door, pulling it open before glancing over his shoulder. "Oh, and *Susanita*?" He waited until she lifted her head to look at him. "I have decided two million is not enough. I want four." With that, he closed the door behind him. She could hear him whistling as he walked away, then calling to the guard stationed outside.

She stood on unsteady legs and made her way to the cracked mirror. Her cheek was already beginning to bruise, turning an angry combination of red and purple. A cut along her cheekbone seeped blood. Where had it all gone wrong? Two years ago, she'd been at the top of her game, a shoo-in for First Lady, married to the man America loved and wanted as their next president. She'd attended dinners given in her honor, was the closest thing this country had to royalty. She'd been beautiful and rich.

Her tired gaze met its reflection. Dark circles marred a pasty complexion. Hair that had once been full and lush now hung lank beside her face. She'd once had a figure most women would die for, but was nothing but skin and bones now. She leaned forward, feathering her fingers across the cheek Garcia hadn't hit, touching the puckered scar that signified everything she had lost. As always when she studied the path of the bullet Luke Barone had shot at her, her anger rose.

It choked her with its intensity and the fiery need to exact revenge. But just as quickly as it came, it dissipated. Two years in a women's penitentiary tended to put things in perspective. She would dearly love to give Lucas and his whore of a wife a taste of their own medicine, but that wasn't to be.

She'd thought she'd be happy living outside the bars of hell, away from the country she'd served for so many years. The same country that had turned on her. Maybe some small part of her had known her downfall would come, because she'd had the foresight to stash enough money in overseas accounts to spend the rest of her life in quiet comfort. Provided Garcia didn't bleed her dry.

She stepped away from the mirror. The past had to stay in the past. The future was all that mattered now. Except there wouldn't be a future unless they could find the paperwork that would allow her to access the accounts. She'd thought they were tucked safely away amongst Bradley's papers, but when Bradley died of a massive heart attack last year, the papers had gone to his trusted advisor, Charles Stewart.

Both she and Garcia had thought it would be simple to retrieve what was rightfully hers.

Until Hope Stewart walked into the middle of it all.

€

Hope woke suddenly, her body tense. For a moment, she couldn't remember where she was. Then her grief came crashing in like huge waves, ripping away everything in its path, leaving nothing but devastation, horror and disbelief. She gulped in air, realizing the whimpers she heard were hers.

John must have left the bathroom light on because shadows danced across the ceiling, while a wedge of light expanded until it failed to penetrate the far corners of the room. It was then she heard the noise. Something other than her pathetic attempt to hold her grief inside.

It was more animal-like. A growl, but human. She sat up and looked around. In the cabin, John had always been a couch-width away and to wake and not find him so close scared her in a way she couldn't name.

The sound came again, followed by a low moan of what sounded like pain.

She pushed off the bed and padded to the door. The hallway was lit only by the moon shining through an end window. She remembered John saying something about sleeping in the guest bedroom, so she followed the hall until she came to a door that was half-open. He was sprawled in the middle of a wide bed, dressed only in boxers, face contorted in pain.

She walked over and leaned down. "John?"

His head moved to the side. Fingers curled into his palm and his breathing became raspy, harsh.

"John?"

His eyes popped open and with an angry growl, he flung his arm out. Surprised, she reared back, his fist barely missing her face. He stared at her with narrowed eyes and a fierce look, as if he would tear her apart if she came any closer.

Seeing in his eyes the last vestiges of a nightmare that refused to release its grip, she advanced slowly. "It's just me," she said softly, touching his bare arm.

He jerked away.

"It was just a dream." She put a knee on the edge of the bed. For every one of her movements forward, he took one away. She'd noticed he didn't like to touch her, but hadn't realized how severe his fears were.

He reminded her of Mugsy.

One of her last memories of her mother was of a sunny summer day when they'd discovered a mongrel dog on their property. It'd been obvious he'd been abused and Hope had wanted to keep him. Her mother had told her the best thing to do was go slow, let him get used to her.

At first, Mugsy had snapped and snarled, never letting her get close. But she'd been persistent and spent hours sitting a good distance from him, talking about anything that popped into her twelve-year-old head. Eventually he'd learned to recognize her voice and one day, not long after, he'd approached, sniffed and shied away. By the end of the summer, he was sleeping in her bed.

She used that same approach with John when she climbed up on the bed. "It's just me." She held out her hands, showing him he had nothing to worry about.

"Angelina?"

Startled by the name, she paused. "No. It's Hope." Another inch forward on her knees, her gaze locked with his. She had a feeling if she gave him time to think, he'd run. So she didn't give him the chance. She pulled the blankets up and slipped underneath, rolling onto her side into the warm spot he'd been sleeping in. "Hold me, John. I need you to hold me."

"Hope—" Her name came out on a strangled groan and she pressed a finger to his lips.

"Shhh. Hold me, that's all I ask. I need your touch tonight." She needed him, needed the comfort of his body close to hers. Needed his strength, and yes, beneath the gruff exterior lay strength and kindness, and oh, how she needed his kindness. Just as, she supposed, he needed hers. "Let's fight our nightmares together." She laid her head on his shoulder, felt the heat penetrate as it chased away the cold inside her. She closed her eyes, pushing away images of her dying father, and draped her arm across John's stomach, snuggling into his side.

She listened to his harsh breathing. The muscles beneath her were rock hard, tense, rigid, until slowly they began to relax. Right before she fell asleep, the shoulder she'd been resting on moved and the arm she'd pinned between them came over her, pulling her closer.

Chapter Ten

John awoke disoriented, his knee sore, with a half-formed headache behind his eyes. He stared at the ceiling as images of Angelina drifted through his thoughts. Over the years, his grief had lessened until there was only a pang now and again in his waking hours. Nighttime proved to be his undoing.

He rubbed his face, scratching at the stubble along his jaw and pushed the painful memories back inside him. Into that deep dark hole where they would fester until it became too much and they'd come clawing out again to haunt him.

Angelina. Some days he wondered if he'd loved her at all. He'd known nothing about her, just that she was kind and kindness had been hard to come by where he'd been. On the days when he could look back with at least a modicum of objectivity, he wondered if he'd made it all up. Not Angelina, she'd been real, but his feelings for her. Had she felt for him as he'd felt for her? Or had he been reaching for something honest and good in a place where honesty and goodness had died long ago, if it'd ever been there at all? Then he would remind himself it didn't matter. She was gone and he was the one who'd killed her.

He flung the covers away and surged off the bed. When he bent to retrieve his jeans, he froze, his gaze glued to the indentation in the second pillow. Denim slipped through lifeless fingers as he straightened and leaned forward to touch the cold sheets on the other side of the bed.

Slowly, other memories emerged. Of Hope standing by the bed. Hope reaching for him, her eyes kind like Angelina's. Her touch healing like Angelina's. He closed his eyes and fisted his hand, pressing it into the soft mattress.

The beast within, the demon that held his nightmares and threatened him every time he tried to get close to a woman, awoke. But this time John fought back, refusing to give in, willing to fight. For kindness, for compassion. For hope.

And when the monster inside him retreated, he opened his eyes and stared at the cooled sheets. She'd crawled into bed with him, held him while he emerged from his nightmare, talked him down from his terror. And he'd held her, too.

When he finally made it downstairs after a quick shower, Hope was sitting on the floor in the middle of Luke's living room, the Christmas presents they'd dumped in John's truck scattered around her. She was staring at them, biting her thumbnail, legs crossed.

Needing caffeine and not quite ready to face her after holding her in his arms most of the night, he ducked into the kitchen, only to find no coffee but a hot pot of water for tea. That's when he remembered coffee made her nauseous. So instead of nuking a mug and taking the chance of making her sick, he poured himself tea and sprinkled in a liberal amount of sugar. Having procrastinated long enough, he made his way to the living room and sat on the edge of the couch, leaning forward, mug of tea held between his spread knees.

She'd obviously gone out to his truck to retrieve the gifts. He probably should have warned her last night not to go out alone, but she'd been so beaten down he'd been afraid to add more fuel to the fire, never thinking he'd sleep later than her. "You okay?"

She nodded but kept her gaze on the brightly wrapped packages. He took a sip of tea and let the silence stretch, having learned that unlike him, Hope didn't like long moments of quiet and she would say something soon. She kept nibbling on her thumb while the other hand played with a red bow. She was wearing the jeans and sweater he'd found her in after she crashed. He didn't know much about pregnant women and what they wore, but he guessed she would outgrow those clothes soon.

"We should buy you some clothes today."

"I want to go to my home."

"Not a good idea."

Her head shot up. Contrary to what he'd been thinking, there was very little grief in her eyes. Oh, it was there, fighting her anger, but so far, the anger was winning. "Why?"

He hesitated, knowing he had to tell her, but wanting to protect her from the harsh reality of what she'd gotten herself into. She had enough to deal with over the next several months. The mind-numbing grief. The questions, the anger, the slow, painful acceptance that her father was gone. Not to mention the birth of her baby, which was huge in and of itself. But she also had a right to know how much danger she was in. "Someone followed us to DC last night."

Her gaze sharpened. "Who?"

"It was too dark to tell. I lost him before we got here, but I don't want you going out alone." He nodded toward the gifts.

"We should call the police."

"No."

"My father was killed," she said vehemently, her voice

rising. “Am I supposed to ignore that?”

“What are you going to tell them, Hope? Your father was killed, yet there’s no body. You witnessed the murder, but fled the scene without calling the police. You disappear for three days, claiming to have lost your memory, but when you visit your dad, it all comes back.”

“Not all of it,” she said without heat, her gaze sliding away.

Something in her tone set his internal alarms clanging. “You remember more?”

She shrugged and played with the red bow again.

“Hope?”

“I remember.”

“You remember everything? Or just what happened the night your father was killed?”

There was a long stretch of silence.

“I remember everything.”

“Tell me.”

“Not much to tell. Basically everything Danny told us. I just remember the specifics.” She massaged her stomach in little circles.

“I’m sorry.” As soon as the words left his mouth he knew they were inadequate. He of all people knew what it was like to lose everything. He should have more to say, but he didn’t.

She blew out a breath. “Yeah. Me too. I loved those kids.”

It was on the tip of his tongue to ask if the school could fire her for such a reason, but he knew they could. Especially in a religious school where morality was ingrained in the pupils’ heads. He wondered about the father of the baby, how he fit into this scenario. If she remembered everything, did she remember his name as well?

She squared her shoulders and seemed to shake off her thoughts.

“Do you see my point about your father?” he asked.

“I don’t like it, but I understand. What are we going to do now?”

“Now we talk. You tell me everything you remember about that night and we go from there.”

A shadow passed across her face, grief and despair and, more than likely, a need to turn away, to ignore what had happened. “Fair enough,” she finally said. “But I want answers from you as well.”

He went still, his barriers slamming into place. “What kind of answers?”

“How do you know my father?”

To stall and to give himself time to think, he settled back into the couch and took another sip of tea. “We both worked for Suzanne Carmichael.”

“Dad was one of Bradley Carmichael’s advisors years ago. I never met the Carmichaels. I was too busy with school and Dad liked to keep that part of his life separate from me.”

John didn’t blame the guy. Something about dealing with Suzanne left a slimy taste in one’s mouth. And after getting to know Hope he would have kept her far from Suzanne, too.

“What did you do for her?” she asked.

“She was my boss in the IATT.”

“Refresh my memory.” Her lips lifted in an ironic smile and John had to grin.

“International Anti-Terrorist Task Force. For a long time we were an invisible arm of the government, a secret weapon so to speak against international terrorism.”

“You were a spy?”

"Sorta." There were things he still couldn't talk about. Not because he didn't want to, but because his security clearance forbade it. But there were also things he didn't want her to know, horrible things. The dark side of humanity he'd just as soon forget but never would.

"Who's Angelina?"

His mug nearly slipped from his hands. "What?"

"Last night you called me Angelina. Who is she?"

"She's dead."

"I'm sorry."

"It was a long time ago." But not nearly long enough. "Tell me about the night you found your father."

Tears leapt into her eyes and he knew the past conversation had been nothing but a diversion to keep her thoughts from her father. He let her talk without interrupting, waiting patiently when she had to pull herself together to go on. She hugged her arms around her middle and stared at the packages in front of her as she spoke in a voice thick with unshed tears.

"So you never actually saw anyone in the house other than your father?" he asked when she finally finished.

She shook her head. "But I felt someone. And I heard them. There's this floorboard by the front door that squeaks when someone steps on it. I heard it that night. It's what made me run out the back door instead of the front."

"Did anyone follow you?"

"No. I jumped in my car and drove to Danny's house. I parked a few blocks away and asked him if I could borrow his car."

"Where'd you get the money?"

"Danny. I'd left my purse in Dad's house and had nothing

on me. Not even a coat. He loaned me the thousand bucks."

"That's an awful lot to ask of a friend." Even as he said the words, he pushed down the irrational spurt of jealousy.

"Danny's a good friend. And I had no idea when I'd be back."

"Then you drove straight to my house?"

She nodded. Her shoulders were bowed and he could tell reliving that night had taken a toll on her. He wanted to question her more. Ask who she thought might have killed her father. He had his suspicions it was Suzanne, but couldn't figure out why she would kill Charles Stewart. Instead, he stood and stretched, willing himself to be patient, to go slow, to remember she'd just lost everything and everyone close to her. "How 'bout we get you some new clothes?"

She struggled to stand and to his surprise, he found himself offering his hand. She seemed a bit surprised too, her gaze flying to his before she accepted his assistance. "Thank you."

A little flustered, he nodded and shoved his hand in his back pocket. What a strange feeling it'd been to touch her without any anxiety.

"I have clothes at home," she said quietly.

"Whoever followed us last night could be watching your place."

"I don't have money for a new wardrobe."

"You can pay me back. Or use Danny's money." The words burned his throat.

"I hate relying on you."

He breathed out a sigh of relief, not understanding why it was so important she not use Webster's money, that she let him take care of her. Hell, some days he couldn't even take care of himself. "I don't mind."

€

After a breakfast of homemade pancakes Hope insisted on making, they headed to the nearest mall. John hadn't been in a mall in years and had forgotten the frenzy of the after-Christmas sales. People rushed around, jostling each other in their hurry, all with a manic light in their eyes that put him on edge. He stuck close to Hope, not touching but brushing against her with each step, keeping his gaze moving, looking for anyone who took more than a passing interest in her.

She entered a maternity shop and, for a moment, John hung back, not wanting to enter, yet not wanting to leave her unprotected either. He compromised by posting himself by the entrance.

At first, Hope was only willing to purchase one outfit. "This is fine," she insisted. "I can make do until I get into my house." She clutched the clothes to her chest like armor.

"We have no idea when we can get into your house. Pick out more clothes."

"Really, John—"

"Fine. If you won't, I will." He searched the store, his gaze skipping over the racks, not knowing where to start but determined she was going to leave with enough clothes to see her through whatever it was they were going to face over the next several days.

He grabbed a winter coat. She was wearing one of his old, ratty coats that was way too big.

"That's not necessary."

"If you don't want to try it on, don't." He didn't know why

he was getting angry. She was proud. That was something he could relate to even though his pride had been stripped from him long ago. He plunked the coat down on the counter and faced her with hands on hips. “Now, are you going to pick some clothes out, or am I?”

They stared at each other for the longest time, waging a silent battle of wills as the wide-eyed store clerk kept her distance.

“I hate that you have to spend money on me. I swear I’ll pay you back.”

“Fine.” He had enough money to spend on her for the next millennium. His cabin was paid for, built with his own hands, and while he didn’t make a fortune with the Sheriff’s department, he had virtually no expenses past utilities and food. He could afford it. And if she insisted on paying him back, he’d open a savings account in her child’s name. As a Catholic schoolteacher, she probably hadn’t made much and now she had a baby to save for. Without insurance, it would be tight for a while. Never mind the fact he wanted to buy her clothes, wanted to help her in any way he could and was oddly hurt she didn’t want to accept his help.

“How about lunch?” he asked as they drove back to Luke’s.

She was staring out the window and had been too quiet for most of the morning. She was keeping a tight rein on her grief and he knew from personal experience that wasn’t good. If she continued this way, she’d end up like him. Lonely and depressed.

“Hope?”

“Hmmm?”

“Let’s have some lunch.” Another moment of silence passed. “Hope. Talk to me.”

"Lunch sounds good."

He pulled into a spot a few blocks from the restaurant he and Luke frequented whenever he made it to DC. "Look, if it's about the clothes—"

"Where do you think they took him?"

"Who?"

"My father. What did they do with his body?"

He ran a hand through his hair and blew out a breath. "I don't know."

"He needs a proper burial."

"I know, sweetheart. And we will. I promise." He had to fight his anger at the injustice, at the complete lack of regard for human life. Why it should surprise him, he didn't know. Long ago he'd come to accept there were people in this world who defied definition.

He couldn't help coming back to Suzanne, but this didn't fit her. Suzanne was out for Suzanne, and wouldn't hesitate to squash whoever got in her way, he was proof of that. But why go after Charles Stewart? And to take the body? That confused him even more. "If you want to go back to Luke's we can."

She sniffed and rubbed her nose with the back of her hand. Again he was reminded of that lost little girl. "No," she said. "I want to go out to eat. For an hour, I want to be normal."

"Fair enough." He turned off the ignition and climbed out of the truck, intent on giving her one hour of normalcy. It'd been a long time since he'd experienced normal himself.

Eclectic shops, trendy boutiques and fashionable restaurants lined the street, bringing with it a wealth of people from all walks of life. Passing one of the restaurants, John had to sidestep a couple that had stopped in the middle of the sidewalk. The woman, a tall brunette, clung to the arm of a blond man dressed in a business suit.

As John skirted them to avoid a collision, Hope slowed. Curious, he glanced at her as she came to a sudden stop. Her face drained of color, her lips turning a sickly gray as her eyes took on a haunted look.

The man had stopped as well and stared at her with pinched lips and narrowed eyes.

"Hope?" John moved in closer, partially blocking her from the other man.

Hope's cold hand found his and squeezed. The brunette tugged impatiently on the other man's arm.

"Hello, Hope," the man said.

Chapter Eleven

Hope wanted to close her eyes, to will a hole to appear in the sidewalk and whisk her away. Even John's presence didn't reassure her. The brunette gave Hope a slow once-over, her gaze assessing, calculating, until it landed on her stomach, then she looked away as if dismissing Hope as any sort of competition. John moved in closer. All she had to do was tell him to get her out of here and he'd take her away. So why didn't she do it?

She licked dry lips. "Jerry."

His blond hair glinted in the sunlight, but lacked the warmth of John's. His brown eyes looked her over, carefully avoiding her rounded belly. She knew him well enough to know he was waiting for her next move, probably wondering if she'd accuse him of something nefarious, like neglect. Or abandonment.

"How've you been, Hope?" His voice was smooth, cool. Elegant. It was what had attracted her in the first place. His suave demeanor had only added to the appeal. But this time his voice grated. And the words struck a pain deep inside.

"We're doing well, Jerry. Thanks for asking." She emphasized the "we" by putting a hand on her belly. His eyes remained steady on hers, as if not seeing the telltale signs meant the baby wasn't there. Well, he had another think coming. The baby was here, alive and well. As if to prove her point, it stretched, then kicked.

He tilted his head toward her. "Glad to hear it."

"Are you?" The words were out before she could bite her tongue.

John shifted, his arm brushing hers.

Something passed through Jerry's eyes. Anger. Accusation. Suddenly she felt drained. And even worse, hurt. It'd been months but the pain wouldn't go away and she wished it was one of the things that had stayed locked in her mind.

"Yes, we're doing very well." She could tell the use of the plural irritated him and she found satisfaction in that.

The woman next to him shifted. Hope held her hand out to her. "I'm Hope Stewart," she said, her gaze sliding to Jerry. "An old friend of Jerry's." Let him sweat it out. Let him wonder what she'd say next. Hope was a little surprised at herself. This was a new side to her, a stronger side she'd never seen before. It could have been John's presence that gave her strength but she believed it was more than that.

It was watching her father die. It was taking control and driving hundreds of miles in search of the elusive John Callahan. It was fighting amnesia and coming out the winner and it was the realization that no matter what Jerry had done to her, she had survived so much more.

For a moment, Jerry's companion stared at her hand as if she didn't quite know what to do with it. Then she shook it limply. "Celia," she murmured, then looked away as if she couldn't be bothered.

Hope smiled at Jerry. His face tightened, then relaxed into a smile that didn't reach his eyes. She could have sworn she saw relief there.

Her smile widened as she turned to Celia. "I've known Jerry for some time. You ever need to know his deep, dark secrets, you just give me a call."

Jerry cleared his throat and rolled his shoulders in his expensive camel-haired coat. "Well, then." He was all false bravado, flashing that killer smile with the dimples that had drawn her to him. "It was nice seeing you." He nodded to Hope, then John, placed a hand on Celia's back and started to walk away.

"Jerry, wait," she called after him. He hesitated before turning around. The smile was back in place, a little strained around the edges. "John and I were just about to eat lunch. Why don't you and Celia join us?"

She waited for his answer, enjoying the way he squirmed beneath the tailored suit and thinly disguised veneer of politeness. "Celia and I just ate. Maybe some other time."

Like when hell freezes over. "Sure."

Jerry hurried Celia down the street. Hope watched him go, the little imp that had egged him on deserting her.

"Remind me never to piss you off," John said.

She shrugged and walked toward the restaurant, suddenly ravenous and craving something with lots of garlic. John fell into step beside her with the good grace not to ask questions. But she knew they were coming, just as she knew she would answer them, dragging out every bit of humiliation that would come with the answers.

"Okay, out with it. Who's Jerry?"

Hope placed her napkin on her lap, taking the time to smooth out all the wrinkles, then play with a frayed edge. The restaurant was a throwback to the seventies and not at all something she would associate with DC. But she liked the red fake-leather booths with the checkered linen tablecloths and the empty bottles of wine with candles stuck in them. It reminded her of that Billy Joel song that started with "bottle of white, bottle of red".

"Hope."

She sighed and shifted her attention to the silverware, turning the fork over and over. "He's Jerry Kemper."

"Never heard of him."

She pursed her lips to keep from smiling. "He'd hate to hear that. He's a rising star in the political arena. Or so he likes to think."

John picked up his glass of wine and took a sip. Hope had ordered water with lemon but hers sat untouched. "Who is he to you?"

Her smile faltered, then faded. "He's..." She'd known talking about this would be difficult, but not nearly this difficult. Obviously, John knew she was pregnant and the father was out of the picture, but telling the whole sordid, ugly tale was a different story. "He's the sperm donor." She watched for John's reaction from beneath half-lowered lids.

He settled back in his chair, his face devoid of expression. "Ah."

Ah? That was it? *Ah?*

"If you don't want to talk about it, we won't."

Her relief was tremendous. But with the reprieve came something else. A need to tell John, to explain. Maybe in the explaining she would understand better. "He's obviously not in the picture anymore. H-he wanted me to abort it." Just saying the words made her feel tainted and the humiliation more acute. Not for the first time she wondered how she could not only have fallen for a man like Jerry Kemper but entertained grand ideas of marriage and a house filled with love and laughter.

John's fingers tightened around the stem of his wineglass. "I'm glad you didn't."

"It'd never been an option." Even if it hadn't been against her religion, it went against her own sense of right and wrong.

"How'd he take that news?"

"Not well."

"I can imagine for an aspiring politician, a child out of wedlock would not be welcome."

She placed a protective hand over her baby, anger rising at the thought that to its father, this baby was nothing but an inconvenience. A liability. "We met at a bar. That should have told me something right there. I don't normally go to bars but Danny had wanted to listen to this hot new band and I was tired of sitting at home on a Friday night grading papers." Geez, how pathetic did that sound? What a loser.

The waiter arrived with a bowl of bread and John reached for a piece. She watched as he tore it apart, then dipped it in olive oil, not seeing the scars on his hand, but the strength. Next to John, she wondered what she'd seen in Jerry.

"He's a good-looking guy," John said. "And I can see where he'd be—" He waved his piece of bread in the air, obviously searching for a word.

"Manipulative," she supplied.

He grinned and her heart did a little flip. She'd never seen him grin like that. He'd laughed before, but there'd always been a cynical edge to it, nothing like this relaxed smile that brightened his eyes. "I was going for something like compelling."

"Maybe at first," she admitted. "He is attractive."

John's face tightened and for a split second she wondered if he might be jealous before she dismissed the thought. He'd done nothing but pull away from her, no way could he be jealous.

"But he's also manipulative. Comes with the territory, I guess. It's all about being a politician."

"So, he found out you were pregnant and wanted nothing to do with the baby."

Her gaze dropped to the table, the words driving a hole through her. "That about sums it up." What an idiot she'd been to believe his smooth words, his practiced touches that set her on fire.

"He's a jerk."

"You don't have to say that. I'm partially responsible. I believed the lies."

"No, Hope." John's look was serious, the smile long gone. "He's a jerk not to see the beauty and the goodness in front of him. To throw it all away on a cold fish like Celia."

She laughed despite the tears burning the back of her eyes, a little stunned at the vehemence in John's words. "I'm not all that good."

John opened his mouth to say something but their food arrived and the conversation ended.

The silence allowed her to think, and as always, her thoughts went to her father. At times, she managed to keep the deep grief at bay, stuffing it down inside, but other times it caught her off guard. Like now. Her dad would like the restaurant John chose. And he would like John. Of course, he'd sent her to John so that was endorsement enough in her mind.

"Tell me how you knew my father," she said between bites.

John pushed his empty plate away. "I didn't. We worked for

Suzanne, like I said, but we'd never met. That's why I'm confused as to why he sent you to me."

She tilted her head and stared at him. He looked relaxed and the look suited him but she doubted he wore it often. He had secrets and a sorrow that went bone-deep. Something that had to do with Angelina. She wanted to hear the whole story but knew it would take a lot of prodding and nagging and by doing so, she'd risk pushing him away. "He was adamant you would protect me and my baby. Maybe he'd heard of you through the Carmichaels."

"Maybe." He crossed his arms on the table and she knew by the look on his face that the conversation was over.

Angelina and Suzanne Carmichael. What had the two women done to him?

She pushed her half-finished plate of spaghetti away, too stuffed to eat any more. "So what now?" Funny how in the course of a few days she trusted him so much. But then, a lot had happened in the past several days, and he'd never once wavered in his promise to help her, even in the beginning when she suspected he wanted nothing to do with her.

What had he been doing on Christmas Day? The thought nagged at her at weird times. Something didn't fit. He'd said he wasn't going to visit family and friends. It was apparent he'd known about the blizzard but hadn't been prepared. As if he hadn't planned on being there for it.

Something cold slithered up her spine and she shuddered at the image of his loaded gun sitting on the kitchen table.

"Cold?" he asked.

"No." She'd always been inquisitive. Sometimes it got her in trouble. Sometimes not. This was one of those times when it probably would. John Callahan was tight-lipped about himself and wouldn't welcome questions from her. But still, she wondered.

The waiter came with the bill and John handed him his credit card. "Now we go back to Luke's," he said, answering her earlier question. "We go over that night again. Go over any enemies your father may have had. We pick everything apart and put it back together until we figure this thing out."

She nodded, not looking forward to any of it, but knowing it needed to be done.

She didn't wait until they got back to the brownstone. "I've thought about it and thought about it, but can't come up with anyone Dad would have made angry enough to want to kill him."

John maneuvered the truck through the streets of D.C. with ease, in direct contrast to the mountain man she'd first encountered. If he'd been an operative for Suzanne, he'd probably been a darn good one with his chameleon-like tendencies to blend in. Since arriving in the capital, he'd changed from the worn jeans and flannel shirts over T-shirts into khaki dress pants and stylish shirts. Today he wore a warm brown mock turtleneck that revealed a well-sculpted body.

"What'd he do after the Carmichaels' fall from grace?" he asked, sliding to a smooth stop at a red light.

"He'd been devastated. His career was ruined, his good name trashed. He hadn't known about the arms deal Suzanne had made or Bradley's partnership with the Saudi prince."

John's hands tightened on the wheel. A tick set up in his jaw and his ruddy complexion faded a bit.

There was something there. Something that had to do with the deal Bradley Carmichael had struck with the Saudi prince to raise the price of oil and line their pockets. Or it could be with Suzanne Carmichael selling arms. Hope tried to remember the specifics, but she hadn't paid much attention at the time, more concerned with her father than with a woman who could do something so horrendous to her country. It had something to do with terrorists in Asia. Or was it South America?

"That had to have been quite a blow," John said as he turned a corner. "Anyone who had anything to do with the Carmichaels either jumped ship or sank with them."

"Unfortunately, Dad sank. I think he was as stunned as the rest of the country at the depth of the Carmichaels' treason. Even though Dad never cared for Suzanne, he and Mr. Carmichael had been friends for years."

"Why didn't he like Suzanne?"

Hope shrugged and shifted in her seat to ease her aching back. It was becoming more and more difficult to find a comfortable position. "He never said. He didn't like to bring work problems home with him. And by the time this all happened, I was living on my own."

"Did he have friends? People who will notice his absence?"

"Unfortunately, probably not. After Suzanne's sentencing, he'd fallen into a semi-depression, rarely left the house, lost touch with the friends who hadn't turned against him." It'd been devastating to watch and worse not to be able to help. He'd always been adamant about not dumping his problems on her. That had been fine when she was thirteen and mourning the death of her mother, but even when she'd become an adult, he'd been tightlipped.

"What did he do for work after that?"

"Not much. He'd take on a case now and then if a neighbor asked. Most didn't ask, though."

"And money? What'd he live on?"

“He said he’d invested well, that his investments were paying off. He even sent me to grad school and bought me a car as a graduation gift.”

She fought the depression trying to pull her down. If she wanted to find her father’s killer, she needed to stay strong, to answer John’s questions and to help in any way she could, but memories were battering her defenses. Her father sitting before his fire, law book on his lap as he dozed. The genuine smile of happiness when she’d visit.

He’d been so proud of her on graduation day, beaming when he’d revealed the brand-new, cherry red Ford Mustang as her gift. That’s why it’d been so hard to tell him about her pregnancy. She’d dreaded a disappointment that had never come.

“Hope?”

She raised her head and blinked. John was half-turned toward her, wrist resting on the steering wheel. His face was bathed in the waning light of day. At first, up at the cabin, she’d been frightened of the harsh lines, but now she’d come to love them.

Love?

Inwardly, she scoffed. No. She hardly knew the man. Though she did like him a lot. He was the only person she trusted in this bizarre situation. And she did enjoy his touch. Maybe because when he bestowed it, she knew it cost him and that made it all the more special. And sleeping with him the night before had been heaven. Her memories had remained buried and for the first time since witnessing her father’s death, she’d slept well.

What would John do if she suddenly said she cared for him? He’d be horrified. Come up with a hundred different reasons why she shouldn’t, none of them dealing with the true reasons. The ones he kept buried in his heart and guarded like a prison fortress.

She didn't think she loved him. But she also didn't doubt she *could* love him. Of course, it would be an uphill battle, trying to fight her way through to his heart. And who said he'd want her in the end? She was a single woman about to have a baby. A lot of men didn't want a ready-made family. Jerry Kemper taught her that.

As soon as the thought entered her head, she felt bad. John Callahan was nothing like Jerry Kemper. But still, she doubted he'd want to raise some other man's kid.

"You ready to go in?"

She shifted her gaze from his face to the brownstone. She nodded and got out while John reached in the back and retrieved her new clothes. Together they walked up the short flight of steps.

When they stepped inside, she pulled up short and John knocked into the back of her, his hand coming to rest on her shoulder to keep her from pitching forward. Her father's gifts still lay scattered on the living room floor, the packages brightly wrapped in laughing Santas and cheery snowmen. Red bows trailed from them, making the place look festive.

"Christmas was his favorite holiday, besides my birthday." Behind her John closed the door and set the packages down. "Why did this happen?"

"I don't know. But we'll find out."

She closed her eyes, picturing her father's body the last time she'd seen him. Where was he? What did they do with him? And *why*? Why would they take his body away?

"Take your coat off. I can make some tea if you want."

But instead of shrugging out of John's coat, she turned and

pressed against him, wrapping her arms around his waist and burying her face in his chest. He smelled of the outdoors, his silk turtleneck soft against her skin as she swallowed past the lump in her throat.

He remained frozen, his arms out to his sides, as if he didn't know what to do.

"Hold me," she said against his chest. She fought the tears of grief. The packages were a horrid reminder that she would never celebrate another Christmas with her father. Never sit in front of a fire sipping hot chocolate and listening to Christmas carols as she told him about her students. Everything had changed and she was only now beginning to realize how alone she was in a world that had turned downright scary.

John's arms slowly came around her, cradling her in his strength and warmth, in the protectiveness she needed so desperately. She would have to soldier on without the one man in her life who had always been there for her, through the grief of the death of her mother, the breakup with her first boyfriend and the trials and tribulations of growing up. But not now. Now she wanted—needed—someone else's strength to draw on.

"What am I going to do?" she asked.

John's hands, at first stiff on her hips, began to move over her back, pulling her closer to him. Her stomach provided an obstacle but he didn't seem to mind. "You're going to survive," he said.

"How?"

"By living one day to the next. And pretty soon you'll look at the calendar and realize days and months have passed and the pain isn't nearly as bad. Then a year will have gone by and the pain will still be there, but you realize it's something you can live with."

She lifted her head and looked at him. His eyes were so

dark and so serious. “How do you know this?”

He shrugged. His hand skimmed her spine and even through the thick coat and sweater, she felt the heat and shivered in response. He had wonderful hands, the scars adding to the greatness of the man. “I just know,” he said.

“Because of Angelina?”

His body stiffened and she felt the need inside him to pull away.

“Because of Angelina.” This time it wasn’t a question. She laid her head back on his chest. “It’s okay.”

He sighed and the sound seemed full of regret. His hands had stopped moving and returned to being stiff. He was still holding her but inside he had retreated.

He pulled back a little and looked down at her, his emotions firmly under lock and key. “Why don’t I make that tea? Then why don’t you open the presents from your father.”

Chapter Twelve

Hope was sitting on the couch when John returned from making tea. He placed a mug on the table beside her, then settled into the opposite end of the couch, his long legs splayed out before him, his big body half-turned toward her.

He was a coffee man. She knew that from looking through the cupboards in his cabin, but ever since she'd said coffee made her nauseous, he hadn't had a sip. He was such a kind, generous man, regardless of what he wanted her to believe.

She fingered the wrapped package in her lap, staring down at the comical Santa with one leg in the chimney, the other firmly planted on the snow-covered roof. She felt like that. One foot dangling over a sheer drop, the other on a slippery slope.

"My mother died when I was thirteen," she said, for some reason wanting John to know her father through her memories. A sort of eulogy. Her dad deserved that at least. "She had ovarian cancer and died four months after being diagnosed. I think Dad and I were still trying to get over the initial shock of learning she had cancer and then, suddenly, she was gone." The pain, like John had said, was still there but dull. What she missed most, especially during her teen years, was a female she could turn to. "At first it'd been hard with just Dad. No matter how much he'd tried to be both mother and father, he couldn't do it."

At the time, shopping for a prom dress with him had been mortifying. Only with age had come the wisdom and the hindsight to realize how much he'd done for her.

She pulled on the ribbon, stretching it taut, then releasing it, watching as it sprang back into its curlicues. "I didn't want to tell him I was pregnant. I was ashamed. Especially when Jerry refused to marry me and have anything to do with the baby. He was so supportive and so excited to be a grandpa." Tears rushed into her eyes. He'd never get to see his grandchild, and his grandchild would never know her father. "So..." She took a deep breath and wiped the tears from her eyes.

John tilted his head toward the gift. "What does the tag say?"

"Baby Boy Stewart." She smiled when she read it.

"He wanted a grandson, then?"

"He never said."

"Open it."

Her hands shook with the realization that this would be the only gift she would give her child from her father. When the wrapping fell away, she lifted the lid and sat back with a grin.

"Don't leave me in suspense," John said.

She lifted out the tiny baseball mitt and laughed.

John smiled with her and toed another box toward her. "Open the next one."

She reached down and snagged the box, finding it harder to bend nowadays. "This one's to Baby Girl Stewart."

"Ah, he was hedging his bets."

"Apparently."

Out of the tissue paper, she lifted tiny pink ballet slippers and set them next to the mitt. Her bottom lip trembled with suppressed tears but she refused to cry. This was a good moment. Bittersweet for sure, but good.

"There're more," John said.

Next she opened a sweater for her and a few gift certificates to her favorite stores. Only one small present remained and she lingered over it, wanting to prolong the moment. While she opened her gifts, she could pretend her father was somewhere, maybe on vacation, and they were separated by miles instead of death, but with the last gift, all pretense fled.

"He's still with you, Hope. In your heart."

Her gaze flew to John's. How did he know what she'd been thinking? How'd he know to say the right thing at the right time?

"Open it," he urged.

Once again her hands shook until the package revealed a sterling silver box, oval in shape, with something engraved on the top.

"'He who has Hope has everything'," she read aloud, her voice shaking with emotion. She dashed at a tear that had escaped. "It's from an Arabian proverb. He who has health, has hope; and he who has hope has everything."

"It's appropriate."

She looked up at him, at the pain that flashed across his face and was gone in an instant. She lifted the heavy silver lid. Once again, tears blurred her vision and her heart beat double-time. She placed the box on the cushion between them and folded her hands in her lap. "I-I can't..."

John reached for it, opened the lid and peered inside. Then he pulled out the folded piece of paper. A letter from her father. She didn't think she could read it, not without falling apart. And it was very, very important she didn't fall apart because she feared she'd never be able to put the pieces back together again.

John's gaze met hers, full of sympathy and understanding.

"I can't read it."

"I think you should." He held the folded paper out to her but she shrank into the cushions, shaking her head. "You need to read it, Hope."

"No I don't." Not yet, at least.

"What if it gives us a clue?"

She stilled. "You think he knew he was going to be killed?"

"We won't know if you don't read it. If you'd like, I'll leave you alone and you can read in peace."

"Don't leave." Her tone turned pleading and she didn't care. Didn't care if John saw her as weak or needy. He simply nodded and she unfolded the letter.

Dear Punkin,

If you're reading this, then something has happened to me. I thought by hiding the letter in the Christmas presents they wouldn't find it. Pretty tricky for a washed-up old man, eh?

She smiled and wiped at her tears. It was as if her father were right here next to her. She could actually hear the timbre of his voice through the words on the paper.

John watched the play of emotions cross Hope's face as she read the letter. She sat with her fist pressed against her mouth, her throat working as if she were fighting nausea. One after the other, tears raced down her cheeks and dripped off her chin and hand.

When she finished reading it to herself, she lowered her fist and cleared her throat. "The beginning's about me, Jerry and the baby."

"You don't have to tell me, Hope."

She shook her head. "You need to know. The money. Suzanne. I know why he died." She hiccupped, holding back a sob. "Suzanne killed him."

She handed him the letter, stood and walked away. John watched her for a few moments, not knowing if he should go to her or read the letter. When she just stood at the window and looked out, he turned his attention to the letter.

Charles Stewart's handwriting reminded him of an EKG reading, all dips and spikes.

I know people thought I had a hand in the whole mess a few years back. But, honestly, I didn't know about the deal with the Saudis. If I had, I would have advised Bradley against it. And Suzanne, I still shake my head over that. What was she thinking? A traitor to her own country, selling weapons to terrorists so they could use them against her own countrymen. It's unforgivable.

Suzanne made a lot of money dealing those arms. The government searched high and low for the profit but could never find it. Then one day it literally landed in my lap. Millions and millions of dollars.

As John read, it took a concerted effort not to fist the paper in his hand, ball it up and throw it into the cold fireplace then flip the switch to incinerate it. What the hell had Stewart gotten himself into?

Not long after Bradley died, I received a sealed envelope from his attorney, advising me that Bradley had named me in the will. Inside were numbers to offshore accounts and credit cards attached to the accounts.

In a letter, Bradley said he was sorry for involving me in the entire mess. He regretted everything he'd done and blamed himself for the ruin of his career and mine. Then he told me about the money. Said if I didn't want it, to give it to the IRS. If anything, they'd implicate Suzanne in tax evasion and make her life a little more difficult.

I swear, Hope, I was going to do it. I was all ready to take everything to the IRS.

Instead, I let myself think about it, play with the idea of keeping it. Then the devil started talking to me. That's the only way I can describe it.

I earned that money with the death of my career. I worked hard for the Carmichaels and had nothing to show for it. Then you wanted to go to grad school and I saw no reason for you to work two jobs to put yourself through when the least the Carmichaels could do was help out. So I used the money. And the car I bought for you was a little gift from them as well.

Over the years I dipped in, nothing major, just a little here and there.

Anger churned in John's gut at Stewart's weakness, at his stupidity in not realizing that what he'd done would come back to bite him in the rear. But mostly at involving his daughter in something she was obviously ill equipped to handle.

Remember a few years back when I opened that safety-deposit box in both our names? I hope you still have the key, but knowing my Hope, you will. Go to the safety-deposit box. Do what you have to. Just don't get mixed up in all this like I did.

If you need help, go to John Callahan. He's a good guy. An honest guy. He'll help you. He has a bone to pick with Suzanne, but he'll help you regardless. Tell him everything if you have to. Dead guys like me can't be proud.

I'm sorry, punkin. Truly, truly sorry.

John guessed that's where he came in. The cleanup team, so to speak. Charles Stewart had used him, used the knowledge that he had an ax to grind with Suzanne Carmichael and bet his daughter's life John would help. And what would have happened if he'd refused? If Hope had never found the letter and Suzanne found her first? Or worse, if she'd arrived at his cabin an hour later?

He tossed the letter on the coffee table and rose. Hope stood at the window, arms wrapped tightly around her as if she would fall apart if she didn't physically hold herself together. Her tears had dried but there were deep lines between her brows, as if she was thinking hard. Or trying not to.

He approached slowly, completely out of his depth. *Thank you, Charles Stewart.* John didn't know how to handle grieving women, angry women or hurt women. And Hope was all three.

Yet, while there was a part of him that wanted to run, a bigger part wanted to stay, to somehow fix this for her. He had to chuckle. Fix things? Him? Hell, he had to fix his own life before he could go tinkering with hers.

He ran a hand through his hair. And when did he go from wanting to end his life to wanting to fix it?

He who has health, has hope; and he who has hope has everything. The proverb fit.

"I hate him," she said, her gaze glued to something outside. Her body shook and he reached out with the intention to touch her shoulder but let his hand drop to his side.

"Right now you do."

"No. I really, really do."

He was so out of his league here. He could use Kate. She would know what to say. But she was in Ohio and besides, this wasn't her problem and Luke would probably shoot him if he dragged Kate into this.

"He paid for my graduate degree with illegal money. And the car..." She sounded bewildered and he wondered what she was going to do when the numbness wore off and the real anger appeared.

"Good people sometimes do bad things. That doesn't make them bad people."

She pursed her lips and he could tell she wasn't ready to listen, but he felt compelled for some odd reason to defend her father. Probably because Hope loved the guy and John didn't want to see her memories tainted with stupid decisions her father had made.

"I wish he'd never met the Carmichaels."

Yeah, well, so did he. But wishing wasn't going to get them anywhere. "He made a mistake. A stupid mistake that got him killed. I imagine in his own way, he thought he was doing good with the money."

"What did he mean when he said you had a bone to pick with Suzanne?"

John drew in a deep breath. Now was not the time to go into that. "Suzanne and I have crossed paths a time or two."

She turned to him, her arms still tightly wrapped around herself. "Tell me, John. Tell me what she did to you. Make me understand."

For a long time, John didn't answer. Couldn't answer. The memories were too close, his anger at what Stewart had done too raw. He'd been manipulated and he didn't take kindly to it. If Stewart were alive, John would have a thing or two to say to the man. But then, if Stewart were alive, John wouldn't be here.

"It happened during the arms deals," he heard himself say. Where the words came from, he didn't know. Why, he didn't know either. Several highly placed psychiatrists had tried to pry the story out of him, claiming it would help his healing process and none had succeeded. "I got a call from Suzanne. She was my boss at the time. Told me about some terrorist activity in

Peru.

"I went. Turns out I was the sacrificial lamb. Suzanne used me to make it look like she was taking action against the People of Light when in actuality she was working with them." He shrugged and let his voice trail off. It took considerable effort to appear nonchalant, like it was all in the past when in reality it was right there before him.

The betrayal had been overwhelming. Before he'd learned the truth, he'd been able to console himself with the fact that what he'd done, what he'd endured, had been for his country, to make the people of the United States a little safer. That belief had been blown out of the water the day Luke called with the true story of Suzanne's betrayal.

It had been the beginning of the end for him.

Hope's eyes had gone soft with pity and horror. The horror he could take. The pity he could not.

"It's over and done with, cupcake. No big deal."

"Why do you call me cupcake when you're trying to push me away?"

"Do I?"

"Yes. It doesn't work. Only makes me want to get closer. I'm sorry for what Suzanne did to you."

"Don't be." He felt the walls closing in on him, his barriers slipping into place, divorcing him from the feelings battering at the defenses he'd learned to erect years ago. He mourned that Hope stood on the other side of his fortification even while he understood the need for it. "I don't need pity."

She shrugged. "I can't help it. It's what I feel. Get over it, Callahan."

Get over it. If only he could.

"You say good people sometimes do bad things. Are you in

that category?"

Relief twisted inside him. For a minute there, he'd thought she was going to want to delve into his stay in the hellhole in Peru. "Maybe."

"What bad things have you done?"

He could think of several. Completely against his will, his feet took a step closer to her. Her lips parted, rosy red from her biting the lower one. His need sprang forth, inappropriate and totally unexpected. He couldn't decide if he wanted her because he hadn't had a woman in years or because she was Hope. A combination of both, most probably.

"Why do you think he did it?" she asked.

John stepped back and cursed himself for being an idiot. Here he was fighting the need to kiss her when she was struggling with her father's deception and death.

"He said why he did it. Weakness. Revenge."

"It wasn't worth it."

"Revenge rarely is."

"Is that why you never went after Suzanne?"

He shrugged. For a long time, he didn't have the energy to go after her, because he'd been concentrating on surviving and healing. Then he just didn't care. About anything.

"What bad things have you done?" she asked again.

"This isn't about me, Hope. This is about your father."

"My father's dead." Grief flashed across her face, but she contained it.

"Yes, and we need to find out who did it." He was desperate to get the conversation back on track. Hope had a way of derailing him, making him think of things other than their purpose. He knew she did it as a defense mechanism against the emotions battering at her.

"We will. You will. I trust you."

"Don't." He took another step back, his hand going out in a motion to stop her words.

"Why does that scare you?" She tilted her head, the waterfall of hair sliding over her shoulder and shimmering in the late-afternoon sun spilling in from the window.

"It doesn't scare me. It's just not wise to trust me."

"My father seemed to think it wise."

"Hope, please—"

"What were you doing the day I crashed on your mountain?"

Chapter Thirteen

John suddenly had an urgent need to be outside, to get away from the walls that continued to close in on him. Nausea clawing its way up his throat, he took another step back, but Hope matched it with a step forward, determination etched in every line of her beautiful face.

"Don't go there, Hope." His voice sounded strangled, panicked.

"What were you doing that day?"

"Walking."

"On Christmas?"

"People take walks every day, even on Christmas."

Those aquamarine eyes, now more like lasers drilled into him, reading his thoughts, seeing things he didn't want her to see. "Knock it off."

"Knock what off?"

He licked his lips. "Don't do this. Don't go there."

"What were you doing that day?"

"I told you—"

"Walking. I don't believe it. Tell me, John."

He closed his eyes and tilted his head back, the pain overwhelming. *Damn it.*

"What would have happened if I hadn't shown up?"

He lowered his head and looked at her, unable to mask the darkness that lay inside.

"Oh, John." Hope lifted her hand, cupped his cheek and rubbed her thumb across his face. He leaned into the caress and closed his eyes. She was so warm and he was so cold. They were like day to night. Sunshine to darkness.

Her other hand cupped his other cheek and he nearly groaned at the contact. Her skin was so soft. So real. For too long he'd denied himself the simple pleasure of human touch.

"Open your eyes, John."

He stared into hers. Once again they were brimming with tears, but this time for him. It nearly buckled his knees.

"I'm sorry for whatever happened to you," she whispered, a shaky smile pulling at her lips. "I'm sorry for whatever it is you've been living with all these years."

He couldn't speak. He was too busy fighting his own tears. Tears he'd refused to shed after the horror of Angelina's death. Hope went up on tiptoes and leaned forward, brushing her lips against his. Shocked, he reared back, but she held tight.

"Don't," she said. "Don't pull away."

He opened his mouth to say something. He didn't know what. To his horror, the tears started falling.

"Oh, baby." Hope gathered him closer, wrapping her arms around his neck. Leaning over, he buried his head in her shoulder, took her in his arms and wept like a baby. For Angelina, for the wasted years, for the pain, both physical and mental. Hope crooned to him and rocked him while he continued to cry. When the well had run dry, he wiped his eyes with the back of his hand and looked away, embarrassed.

"Uh-uh." She pulled his hands toward her. "Don't go hiding

behind that gruff exterior again," she commanded.

"I'm sorry." It was all he could think to say. What was a guy supposed to say after breaking down and crying like a baby all over the woman he was supposed to be protecting?

"No, John. Don't be sorry. Never again. Look at me."

Reluctantly, he slid his gaze to hers but found she was smiling. He hadn't seen her smile yet, not like this. Not with her eyes. Enraptured, he reached out and touched her cheek.

"I like that," she said.

"Like what?"

"Your touch."

He pulled away and curled his fingers into a fist. She grabbed his hand and held it tight.

"Touch me again."

Oh, Lord. "Hope, it's not a good idea."

"Yes it is. Here." She pulled his hand up to her face, ran his fingers across her cheekbone, her chin, her lips. Like a blind person who could suddenly see, he felt. Brushing the tips of his fingers across her lips, feeling the moisture, the softness. Like rose petals. Only better.

"You can kiss me," she whispered, her words vibrating on his fingers, her breath caressing his knuckles.

He stared at her mouth for the longest time, then slowly lowered his head until he could feel her breath on his own lips, mingling with his ragged breathing.

"Kiss me," she repeated.

He closed the distance between them, brushing his lips against hers. Soft didn't begin to describe it. Heaven.

Hope tilted her head and moved forward so the kiss became more than a touching of the lips. Deeper. And a hell of a lot more scary. He stomped down on the rising panic.

Hope opened her mouth and his tongue found its way home. He crushed her to him and she mewled, the sound resonating inside him.

He felt alive, and it was a damn good feeling.

Hope pulled away first or else he would have kept going. She stared up at him, eyes shining with laughter, face flushed. He touched her hair, running his hand through the silky strands, feeling the softness there as well. Was she soft everywhere?

He reined those thoughts in. It was one thing to kiss her, another to think about making love to her. To drive home that point, the baby kicked. Hope was pressed so tightly to him, he felt it against his hip and looked down in shock.

She laughed and pressed his hand to her stomach where all kinds of movement was going on.

“What’s it doing in there?” he asked in awe.

“I wonder that myself sometimes. I think cartwheels.”

“It’s...amazing.”

Her expression softened. “It is, isn’t it?”

“I can’t imagine someone giving this up. Jerry Kemper is a fool.” The minute the man’s name left his lips, John cursed himself for being the fool and bringing the man up, but Hope only laughed.

“He is,” she agreed.

He pulled out of her arms to give himself a chance to breathe, to get his body under control. But he couldn’t resist running his hand down her arm, touching her one last time. Somewhere the panic inside him slumbered.

“I want to make love to you.” He surprised himself by voicing the words and quickly tried to backpedal. “I mean...

Damn, I'm sorry. I shouldn't have said that."

She grinned and pressed a finger to his lips. His tongue flicked out. She tasted so good—salty and warm—that he couldn't resist.

"Make love to me, John."

He shook his head and took a step back, breaking contact, missing it immediately. "Not a good idea."

"Why?" She stood alone, her hands at her sides, the late-afternoon sun pouring in behind her. Like an angel.

Like Angelina.

His gut tightened and he ran a hand through his hair. But Hope, being Hope, wasn't taking no for an answer. He should have figured. Maybe had even...hoped. She invaded his personal space, wrapping him in her warmth.

"Tell me what you're thinking." Her voice turned sultry, sexy and oh-so tempting. His body responded, leapt to life in a way it hadn't in such a long time.

"Hope—"

"Give me one night," she pleaded. "One night to hold off the memories that will haunt me forever. Give me something good in all this bad. You said good people make bad choices. But don't good people also make good choices?"

He stared at her, his body a whirling mixture of needs and demands that superseded all rational thought. One night. What he wouldn't give for one night with Hope.

Little did she know—or maybe she did—that he too needed to hold off the memories that haunted him. Needed something good in all the bad that had become his life. "Are you sure?"

"Absolutely." She held out her hand. He took it and they stood there like that, linked by their fingers and so much more.

They turned together and headed into the bedroom.

Moonlight filtered in through the gauzy curtains in the guest bedroom. Hope turned to face John, excitement and apprehension in her expression. He faltered, wondering if this was the right thing to do. What if he failed? What if he discovered he couldn't do it? Touching her wasn't a problem anymore, but being inside her, being close to her in the most intimate, personal way might be.

And what if, once he started, he couldn't stop? It'd been a damn long time and he feared he wouldn't be able to control himself.

She smiled. Weak light barely highlighted one side of her face. He couldn't resist touching her with his fingertips, memorizing through feel alone the warmth of her skin.

She did the same, her fingertips floating from his face to his chest where his muscles flexed with every brush of her hand.

"Touch me," she whispered. Her hands wandered from his shoulders to his biceps until they found his fingers. John leaned down, taking her lips in a tender kiss that required all his self-control to contain. He wanted to back her against the bed, lay her down and yank her jeans off.

"I'm scared," he said against her mouth, ashamed to admit his fear, yet needing to tell her.

"Oh, John." She cupped his face, stared into his eyes. It helped that he saw no pity. "I'm scared, too."

Her admission made him weak in the knees and he smiled. "We're like two teenagers. Like it's our first time."

She chuckled and patted her belly. "Well, we know it's not mine."

"Mine either."

Her smile faded. "We'll be all right, you know."

"Yes." Yes, they would be all right. They would heal. He wouldn't have thought that three days ago, or even two. "Because of you," he said.

She shook her head. "Because of us."

His eyes burned and he realized he was damn close to crying again. What this woman did to him. "Tell me." He cleared his throat. "Tell me if I'm too rough. Tell me if you want me to stop."

"I trust you. But I'll tell you."

She stepped back and, in a swift move, pulled her sweater over her head. He groaned at the sight of her breasts spilling over the top of her bra. Of course, he'd seen them before, when he'd undressed her after the wreck, but this was different and this time he looked. They were even bigger than before. Fuller. Ripe. Ready for the baby, her nipples large and erect. He'd known men who thought pregnant women sexy and had never understood the concept until now. Her pebbled nipples pressed against the thin silk and his hands itched to touch them, his mouth watered to taste them. He brushed the back of his hand against one. Hope gasped and arched forward, her eyes closing halfway. "Oh, yes. Please touch me."

Touch. His knees were ready to buckle. He was so hard it hurt but he forced himself to go slow, monitoring every movement, testing his restraints and pushing the envelope with each touch, each thought, each fantasy. He fumbled with the front clasp of her bra until her breasts sprang free and she moaned, the sound pounding at his self-control. "Oh, that feels so good," she whispered.

He was finding it harder and harder to pull in a breath. He cupped her breasts, weighing each one in his hands. The skin was so soft and supple.

He flicked his thumbs across an engorged nipple. Her head

fell back, exposing the long column of her neck. He nibbled on her skin. “Oh, John.”

He chuckled, or at least he thought did. He couldn’t tell through the sensual haze that had him all wrapped up. He lowered his head and flicked out his tongue, wetting a nipple, then taking it in his mouth. She grasped his head between her hands and countered his sucking movements with a thrust of her hips. Each suck, each flick of his tongue made her go faster, her belly brushing against his.

Her breath became ragged and he switched breasts, his hand going to the one he’d just left, massaging it as he pleasured the other. Little sounds escaped her throat, whimpers of need that drove him on. Then he lifted his head, his hands going to her waist as he backed her toward the bed.

She lay on her back and John loomed above her while she wrestled with the zipper of his pants, brushing her fingers against an erection so hard it pained him and he had to hiss in a breath as his hips automatically lunged forward. With the zipper down, she wiggled her hand inside his underwear and her fingers encircled his hardness. He grabbed her hand to stop her.

“How are you?” he asked.

Her eyes flew to his, tinged with amusement. “Just fine. How are you?”

“Desperate.” He smiled. “Are you sure you’re okay?”

She squeezed and his eyes closed. “Hope.” His voice sounded strangled, pained.

“I’m fine, John. More than fine. But I won’t be if you don’t let us continue.”

He knew he was being stupid. Overly cautious. But the last thing he wanted was to hurt her.

"Can I have my hand back?" she asked on a laugh.

"Please." His head fell forward as she pumped him. Each stroke brought him closer to the brink. His breath came fast, then faster as he thrust into her hand. He could feel himself grow harder, the pressure building to an explosive conclusion, but he didn't want to come this way.

"Stop." The word was strangled. For a moment he remained perfectly still as his penis throbbed against her hand. "That was close," he whispered, leaning down and brushing a kiss across her forehead. He pulled her hand away and fell beside her, rolling her toward him.

"Is it safe?" he asked as he caressed her belly. The skin was tight, underneath hard as a rock. The baby seemed to be sleeping.

"Perfectly." She wrapped her arms around his neck and rose up, kissing his lips, his nose, his cheeks and chin while he worked on pulling her jeans off.

"I want you so bad it hurts," he said, his breathing once again going ragged.

"Me too." She kicked off her jeans and worked on his pants. Both pants and boxers came off together and his penis sprang free.

"I don't have protection," he said, cursing silently. He'd never even considered needing it.

"It's not like I can get pregnant." She arched her back, silently begging for his touch, but he held back.

"I haven't been with anyone for four years."

Her gaze flew to his but it was too dark to read the expression in them.

Embarrassed by his declaration, he looked away and cleared his throat. "I guess what I'm trying to say is that I'm clean. I've... I've been in and out of the hospital since then and tested for everything known to man."

She leaned down, her elbows on either side of his head. "Someday we're going to talk about this. About what happened to you. Not now, though."

"No. Not now." Not ever if he had his way.

She ran her fingers through his hair. "I'm glad it's you."

Her breasts brushed against his chest and he felt himself harden even more. Distracted, he watched the way they swayed. "Glad what's me?"

She bit his shoulder and his hips rocked.

"Jesus, Hope."

"Glad it's you I'm making love to."

He pulled his gaze from her swinging breasts to her face. "Me too," he said.

She touched his shoulder where she had bit him, rubbing the tender skin. "I'm clean. Jerry's the only one—"

He touched her lips with the tip of his finger, having no desire to hear about Jerry Kemper. "Enough said." He nudged her off him and shrugged out of his shirt. As she lay on the bed, her hands brushed his back. He knew the moment her fingers encountered the thick, raised skin because she stilled. He paused, fighting the instinct to hide behind the walls of his defenses.

He'd seen the scars. They weren't pretty and, worse, they were a reminder of all that his life had been. And what it couldn't be. They stared at each other in the silence of the night, their breathing in sync, their gazes locked on each other. He fully expected her to either ask questions or get up and walk away.

She continued her exploration of his back, stopping for a

moment at each strip of scarred skin to investigate it before moving on.

"You're a beautiful man," she whispered. "Both inside and out."

His chest tightened with a feeling that scared the crap out of him. He battled it down, forcing it into submission and away from his thoughts. It was a mixture of tenderness, protectiveness and he could have sworn love. Of course he was mistaken.

"Make love to me, John Callahan."

She smiled and slowly he pushed his way inside her. She was tight but so wet he slid in easily as if they were made to be together. Her face contorted and he stopped. "Am I hurting you?" He had to hold his breath and battle the urge to push forward. He began to pull out but she shook her head and grabbed his hips to stop him.

"Don't," she said.

"I don't want to hurt you."

"You could never hurt me, John."

"Oh, Hope." If she only knew just how much he feared hurting her.

She winced again. He gathered her in his arms as best he could and rolled until she was on top, looking down at him. "Better?"

She smiled, her hair falling forward, tenting them. It brushed against his nipples and the feeling was erotic. Sensual. "Much," she said.

She rose up, then came down. Up, then down until he was gritting his teeth, barely holding on to his weakening control. Her heavy breasts swayed and he touched the tip of one, inciting a moan of approval from her.

Using both hands, he pressed her breasts together and raised his head to lick and suck. Hope grabbed his hair and pushed her chest into him, moving faster until he was just at the brink, then the minx would slow, giving him time to catch his breath.

The little sounds she made drove him crazy, pushing him closer to release, but he refused to go without her. Hope leaned forward, braced her hands on his chest and moved faster, crying out as she came. She milked his orgasm from him, her muscles clenching around him, squeezing. He groaned as he came inside her, thrusting deep. His release was more than physical, more than mental, bordering on spiritual. He knew, after tonight, that he would never be that same man who had dragged an unconscious Hope from her car.

Chapter Fourteen

Suzanne tried to tune the battery-operated radio, listening for any mention of her escape. Damn Manco. She was paying him two—correction, *four*—million dollars. The least he could do was put her in a decent hotel instead of an abandoned one with no electricity or running water.

Except for a small blurb stating the manhunt was ongoing, there was nothing. She'd been replaced by a snowstorm that had crippled Denver. At one time, she'd made headline news on a daily basis and no snowstorm would have dared upstage her. Sometimes she longed for that part of her life. It was still a little surreal she had to spend her energy on more crucial pursuits, like staying one step ahead of the authorities and keeping Garcia from killing her. She wrapped her arms around her middle and rocked back and forth.

It had all seemed so easy. All she'd had to do was use the complicated snail-mail system Garcia had set up when she first started selling arms to his organization. If the guards at the prison monitored her mail, they'd see nothing but an innocuous letter to an old friend. Never would they suspect they were reading code for a prison escape.

The lure of two million dollars had been too much for Garcia to ignore. And, being the greedy terrorist, he'd instantly replied. He'd do anything for money. He'd do anything his twisted mind thought was entertaining, and Garcia's idea of entertainment was worlds apart from hers.

Images of a beaten and nearly comatose John Callahan instantly came to mind. Callahan's wounds had been inflicted by Garcia for the sheer enjoyment. He'd wanted revenge against her for involving the US in his business and potentially exposing their agreement.

Garcia had no qualms torturing women as well. There'd been that prison cook. What was her name? Angela? No, Angelina. Suzanne had never seen what Garcia had done to her, but she'd heard stories that stood her hair on end. She didn't hold much faith in God and didn't believe in His revenge, but if she did, this would be a perfect example. She was caught in the clutches of her own making, having handed over the reins of power to a man who would easily, and without second thought, eliminate her.

She heard voices outside, first muted then growing louder. She slid off the bed and tiptoed to the window to peek through the crack in the draperies. Outside the door, Garcia was deep in conversation with his sidekick, Ramon. Tómas exited the room beside her, suitcase in hand, and headed for the car.

She yanked the door open. "Where's Tómas going?"

Garcia glanced around but there was no one about. He'd picked her prison well away from civilization. "Get inside, Susanita, before you are seen."

"Where's Tómas going? Why does he have his suitcase?"

This had been her worse fear. That Garcia would get tired of waiting for his money and return to Peru. She was well aware he wouldn't leave any evidence behind. Namely, her.

He hustled her into the room. Ramon followed, shut the door behind him and leaned against it. Suzanne's gaze bounced from the blocked door to Garcia.

"I have business in my country," Garcia said with a Gallic shrug. "It is time I leave."

"You can't leave me here."

Garcia tilted his head, his dark eyes nearly glittering. "I should take you with me?"

"Yes. Take me with you."

His hand whipped out and caught her on the temple, causing her to stumble back. Her vision went white with pain and she cried out.

"You play me for a fool. Two weeks I have been in this country. I risk everything to get you out of prison. You promise payment but so far I have worthless excuses." He advanced on her, spittle flying, face flushed with something that went beyond rage.

Suzanne retreated, feeling the wall behind her with her hands as she slid along it. "Please," she begged. "Please don't go. I'll do anything you want."

With a muttered curse, Garcia pulled out a weapon—a deadly looking Glock with a black barrel. She froze as he checked the slide for ammunition, the schnick of well-oiled metal on metal loud in the quiet room. He balanced the weapon in his palm, and for a crazy second, she wondered if he was going to shoot her with a gun she'd sold to him.

He glanced back at Ramon who nodded. Suzanne lurched forward, fell to her knees as she grabbed Garcia's legs. "Please. Please don't do this, Manco. I'll get your money. Five million. I'll give you five million. You can buy a lot of weapons with that." She'd stashed the money for emergency purposes and damn if this wasn't an emergency.

For a moment, Garcia stared at her in a mixture of horror and curiosity, then he fisted his hand in her hair and lifted her off the ground until she stood on her toes. She winced and wrapped her fingers around his wrist. Tears of pain blurred her vision.

His eyes were fierce, angry and contemptuous. "Talk." He shook his arm and she cried out. "Beg me, Susanita. Beg me for your life."

"Okay, okay." She thought frantically. "Hope Stewart. She has to have friends. Someone she'd run to for help. If we find those friends, we find Hope. And we find the money."

Garcia let go and she stumbled back, rubbing her aching scalp and staring at him with a mixture of hope and fear. "We searched her *casa*. There was *nada*."

"What about an address book? Letters? Tómas and Ramon, they don't read English well, yes? Have them bring all of those things and I'll find someone. I swear to you, Manco, Hope couldn't have disappeared on her own."

Garcia seemed to think for a moment before turning to Ramon. "Tell Tómas to search the *puta's* house again. Tell him what we are looking for. And tell him to hurry. If he's not back in an hour, we kill the woman and get out."

Ramon opened the door and spoke in rapid Spanish, then shut it and leaned against it again. Suzanne sagged against the bureau. She'd bought herself an hour at least.

"Now, *querida*." Garcia stepped closer. "Since I have no money to show for my effort, it is time for you to begin paying your debt." He reached for the fly of his pants. In the heavy silence, the zipper sounded loud and ominous. Her gaze went to Ramon who straightened in interest.

Garcia grabbed her by the hair and forced her to her knees in front of the open fly of his trousers. She winced at the pain in her scalp and her stomach turned in dread. "You said you would do anything, yes?"

"Y-yes." What pride she had left, evaporated. She'd do

anything to stay alive.

Anything.

€

Hope shifted again. John rolled onto his back and stared at the shadows of the pre-dawn sun on the ceiling. He was still astounded he'd actually made love to her without drawing back. Without turning away. Without losing control. This was the first morning he'd awoken free of the burden that had become so heavy he could barely make it out of bed in the morning. He felt like a whole man and not some freak with a yawning black hole inside him.

Hope moved again, then turned on her side and tucked her hands under her cheek.

"You okay?" he asked.

"It's the baby. My back's been bothering me too." Under the covers, her hand snaked up to his chest and rested there. "Quit frowning," she said. "It's been like that for the last month or so."

He covered her hand with his. "Tell me about it."

"About being pregnant?" Her voice sounded surprised in the dark.

"My sister had three before..." He cleared his throat. "Before I left. She complained a lot. Is it really that bad or was she playing for some sympathy?"

"It's not that bad, but then you need to ask me in three months when I'm bigger than a whale and can't get around."

His smile slipped. He probably wouldn't be around in three months and the thought of Hope all alone and in pain had his gut clenching.

"At first," she said, "feeling the baby move was...weird. Like little bubbles. It's hard to describe. But lately, those little bubbles have graduated to kicks and stretches. Sometimes I think he's wearing boxing gloves." She took his hand and moved it to the side of her stomach where the little devil was sparring even as they spoke. Awed, he kept his hand there, eagerly awaiting the next kick. There was a smile in the tone of her voice. "But I love it," she said. "If I don't feel a kick every now and then, I worry."

When it was obvious the baby had expended all its energy and had gone back to sleep, Hope drew their hands out from beneath the sheets and raised them up. The morning light had strengthened, filtering through the gauzy curtains and bathing the room in lighter shades of gray.

Remarkably, he felt no compulsion to pull away as she studied his scars. She kissed his knuckles and laid their clasped hands between them. "Tell me what happened."

There was no dread inside him at her words. Last night he'd known the question would come and had dreaded it, but this morning was different. This morning *he* was different. "Like I said, Suzanne called me down to Peru to help with some terrorist activity that supposedly threatened the United States. Apparently she was playing both ends, appeasing the president by sending me into a trap while making her deal with Garcia." Hatred, strong and putrid, roiled inside him. He did this every now and then, went through periods of hatred, wanting to hunt down Garcia.

"Who's Garcia?"

He forced himself to remember, forced the words past a throat quickly closing. So much for being different. Baby steps. He had to accept that his return to normalcy would take place in baby steps. "Manco Garcia is second in command of the People of Light, a terrorist organization in Peru." A man who possessed a vitriolic hatred for Americans but somehow justified dealing with them when it came to procuring weapons for his organization. John had encountered many different people in his line of work, but no one came close to the evil living inside Garcia.

"So Garcia kidnapped you and held you hostage?"

"Yeah." It was as simple and as complicated as that.

"How long were you there?"

"They say three months."

"They say? You don't remember?"

"I don't remember much." Just the humiliation and degradation. The nearly daily beatings. The prayers to God to let him die. And Angelina.

He'd been at the end of his rope, hanging on by some stupid life force, when Luke had arrived, negotiating to take John's place. What a stupid fool Barone had been, but John owed him his life. Some days he didn't know if he should curse Luke or thank him.

"Tell me about Angelina."

He stiffened, his hands ceasing their endless motion on her arm. He closed his eyes to stop the memories, but all he could see was blood and Angelina's body thrown carelessly into the corner of his cell. At first, he'd thought he'd killed her. His hands had been bloody and, like a roadmap, the trail of blood had gone from him to her.

Seeing her battered body mutilated almost beyond recognition had pushed his mind over the edge. He'd started screaming. Guards stood at the door and laughed as one lone figure stayed back from the rest, his beady eyes taking it all in, his face impassive.

John had crawled to her, gathered her close to his chest

and rocked her cold, lifeless body. Her blank eyes had stared up at him, clouded with the terror of what she'd endured because of him. If he hadn't talked to her, if he hadn't touched her...

Cool fingers touched his cheek, brushing away hot tears. "It's okay," Hope murmured.

With the images of Angelina in his mind, he quickly let go of Hope and tried to scoot away, but Hope tugged him close.

"I'm sorry," he whispered. "I can't..." He couldn't tell her, couldn't voice the horror. Didn't want to burden her with the mental image of what had become of a wonderful, bright, cheerful woman who had made the mistake of caring for him.

"I'm not Angelina," she said, her voice strong. "Look at me, John." She clamped her hand on his chin and turned his head her way. "Look at me. What do you see?"

He saw eyes spitting flames, a face fierce with determination, rosy lips murmuring his name. He saw hope.

"I'm not Angelina. Nothing's going to happen to me."

Slowly he relaxed against her, feeling a determination he hadn't felt since he'd first been taken prisoner. He might never be the man he once was—Garcia had taken too much from him—but he could still be a man.

When he emerged from a steaming shower later that morning, Hope was at the oven, flipping bacon with a fork, wearing an old flannel shirt of his that came almost to her knees. She'd rolled the sleeves several times but they still hung below her elbows.

He stepped up behind her and pulled her against a sudden erection. He slipped his hands beneath the shirt and cupped breasts that seemed heavier and fuller today than they had last night. One hand rubbed the smooth, tight skin of her stomach and felt a small kick in response. He chuckled, his lips pressed against the back of her neck.

"I thought I bought you clothes."

She tilted her head to the side and he nuzzled, inhaling the scent of bacon and coffee. "I liked this shirt better."

"Thanks for the coffee," he said against her skin.

"You're welcome. All I had to do was hold my nose while I scooped the grounds into the coffee maker."

"I appreciate it."

She placed plates of bacon and eggs on the table and motioned for him to sit while she poured his coffee then joined him. "Tell me about these overseas accounts," she said as she scooted her chair in. "I don't understand how my father could use an account Suzanne opened."

John collected his thoughts, trying to remember all he'd been taught. "In the United States, if you deposit a large amount of money into your account, the IRS requires documentation and forms to be filled out for tax purposes." He dug into his eggs and took a bite, then continued after swallowing. "But in certain overseas countries, there's none of that. I think the type of account Suzanne has is untraceable. Basically, whoever holds the paperwork, whoever has the debit card with the PIN, owns the account."

"And that would be me." She pushed her full plate away.

"That would be you." He pushed the plate back at her. "Eat."

She picked up her fork and spread the eggs around on her plate.

"Eat, Hope. Worrying isn't going to help the baby."

She took a small bite, puckered her mouth and bolted from the kitchen. Stunned, John sat there as her chair clattered to the floor. But when he heard her in the downstairs bathroom, gagging, he ran after her.

“I’m okay,” she said, her head hanging over the toilet.

He knelt beside her and pulled her hair out of the way as her stomach heaved again. “What happened?”

She retched. “Morning sickness.”

That was crap and he knew it. They’d woken up together several days in a row now and not once had she had any morning sickness. This was fear, plain and simple.

He grabbed a washcloth and soaked it in cold water, then washed off her face as she knelt on the floor in front of him, her face turned up to him. When he was finished he lifted her to her feet. She was a little wobbly at first. “Will you be okay?”

“A few crackers and I’ll be fine.”

She turned in his arms and hugged him tight, her stomach pressing against his pelvis. “I don’t want this to end,” she whispered, her words broken with emotion.

“Throwing up?” He tried to laugh but his joke fell flat and he held her tighter. “What if I promise it won’t?”

She pulled back and stared at him with a serious expression. “What are you saying?”

“We’ll talk about...us...after this is over.”

“Will it be over?” She had dark circles under her eyes, her complexion was pasty, and between them the baby kicked up a storm.

“Yes.” His answer was more forceful than his feelings. Truth was, he didn’t know what the next few hours held for them and he didn’t quite trust himself yet. His training was rusty, his instincts long unused. She smiled and he saw the trust in her eyes. A trust he hoped to God he didn’t betray.

Chapter Fifteen

John raised his eyebrows in surprise. "You put it in the freezer?"

"Dad said to put the safety deposit key somewhere safe and I remember watching an Oprah show where someone mentioned freezing your credit cards in ice. That way if you want to use them you'll have to chip through the ice and by then you'd have second thoughts." Hope shrugged. "I thought it was a good idea."

He leaned over and kissed her on the nose, unable to resist because she was so damn beautiful and resourceful.

"Are you sure you can get in the house?" she asked.

"I've picked bigger locks than the one on your front door, Hope. I'm sure."

She bit the corner of her lip, looking concerned. He knew she didn't like him leaving her and he hated that he had to, but someone had to retrieve the safety-deposit key and he sure as hell didn't want her going with him. More than likely Suzanne had Hope's house staked out.

"There's something that's been bothering me," Hope said.

"What's that?" She'd gained a little of her color back since getting sick but she still had dark circles under her eyes that worried him.

"Suzanne Carmichael."

The name, dropped into the middle of his thoughts, was like a bucket of ice water tossed on his head. "What about her?"

"If she escaped from prison, she wouldn't want to be traipsing all over Maryland looking for me. She'd want to lay low."

John had thought of that too, but had kept his suspicions to himself. He should have realized Hope would realize the same thing. "I think she's working with someone," he admitted.

"Who?"

"That's what I can't figure out. Her few friends have left her, not willing to ruin their own careers by being seen with her."

"Did she have a lover?"

"Yeah, but he's dead." Shot and killed by Luke when the man tried to kill Kate.

"Could she have met someone in prison?"

"I suppose." He hadn't been able to figure out who Suzanne could be working with and that made going to Hope's house all the more dangerous. He had no idea what he'd be walking in to.

"What are you going to do with the key once you get it?" she asked.

"I'll come back and pick you up. We'll go to the bank, see what your dad left us. If it's the paperwork for the offshore accounts, then we go to the authorities and turn everything over to them. That will get the killer off our backs."

"What about Suzanne? She's still out there. And my dad." Tears filled her eyes but she blinked them away. "We still don't know where his body is."

John cupped her chin. "Hope, we may never find your father."

Her bottom lip trembled and she sucked it between her

teeth. "I don't know if I can live with that."

He understood, but he was also realistic. The chances of finding her father's body were slim, especially if it hadn't been found by now. Someone had gone to a lot of trouble to hide Charles Stewart and if John didn't find that someone, then Stewart's body might never be found. He kissed her. "Do you remember how to activate Luke's alarm system?"

She nodded. John hesitated. For nearly six days, they hadn't been out of each other's sight. To leave her felt like a betrayal.

"How are you feeling?" he asked.

"Better."

He studied her face. "You sure?"

"I'm fine, John. The crackers helped."

"Eat some more. And rest. And don't answer the door no matter who it is." He opened his mouth to say one last thing, but then closed it with a snap when he realized the words that were about to come out were *I love you*. He wasn't ready for that yet. Maybe when this was over and they sat down to talk. Maybe when he had time to think about it without dead bodies to find and escaped convicts on the loose. Maybe then.

€

Suzanne searched through Hope's address book and correspondence one more time. According to the information Tómas and Ramon had returned with, Hope Stewart had a few friends she worked with but only one true friend. Daniel Webster.

She shifted and winced, muscles and torn skin sending up a protest of pain. The door opened and she jumped, scattering papers across the bed. Garcia entered, looking as unrumpled and perfectly put together as he had when he'd left to find Webster. Ramon followed and took up his place in front of the closed door with his arms crossed. His white shirt was spattered with what looked like blood and his hair was a mess.

Garcia paced in front of the bed, hands deep in his pockets as he stared at the floor. "She is with John Callahan."

Suzanne blinked. John Callahan. There was a name from the past. For some reason she'd thought he'd died a few years back—after the whole Barone debacle. How in the hell had Hope Stewart found him? And why? "Where are they?" she asked.

"They visited Webster two days ago. The Stewart woman had no memory."

Suzanne's heart sank. "So she may not know she has the papers. Or if she has them, she doesn't know what they are."

"Webster said she made no mention of money or papers. Yet she must have them. Why else would she run?" He pounded his fist into his open palm. "John Callahan would know what the papers mean."

The implication sank into Suzanne's weary brain. Callahan would know. He would go to the authorities. Garcia would never get his payment and Suzanne would never be free.

Garcia leaned forward, pressing his palms into the bed and tipping her forward. "Where would Callahan be, Susanita?"

Desperate and fighting panic, she searched her mind. Damn. John Callahan. This had now become personal with Garcia. Somehow Callahan had managed to win over the heart of Garcia's cook while he'd been imprisoned. Garcia hadn't taken kindly to his niece falling for an American spy and he'd killed her. Slowly. Ruthlessly. Then threw the body in John's cell. It had nearly broken John's mind. Some said it *had* broken his mind. And it had been the catalyst that sent Luke Barone in after his best friend.

"Querida?"

Lucas Barone. John Callahan's best friend. Lucas who lives in DC. "I think I know where Callahan and the Stewart woman are."

Garcia straightened, cracked his knuckles and stared at her.

"I think they're with Lucas Barone." She began to get excited. A few short hours ago she'd been begging for her life and now she could almost taste her freedom. Of course John would to go Lucas. And Hope would be with John. They hadn't turned the papers in to the authorities yet or it would have been all over the news. There was still hope. Garcia would soon get his money and Suzanne could disappear. No more prison. No more locked doors. No more Garcia.

"This is the same Lucas Barone and John Callahan who escaped my prison, yes?" Something deadly flashed across his face.

"Yes, they're the same." She didn't add that Lucas and his wife had been the ones to send her to prison and destroyed a carefully mapped out life that would have netted her *everything.* Oh, yes. Suzanne could understand unfinished business. "Barone lives in DC," she added, warming to the idea of a little revenge on the way to her freedom.

Garcia nodded as he stared at the floor. His hand went to his chin and he rubbed it with his thumb. He barked out orders to Ramon in Spanish, something about Tómas watching Hope's house while Ramon and Garcia went to visit Barone's.

€

Hope lived halfway between DC and Baltimore, about a thirty-five minute drive from Luke's townhouse. Each mile that slipped between he and Hope had John more agitated and more determined to get in and out of her home and back to her as fast as possible. Amazing that for years he'd lived alone, happy in his seclusion and in six days Hope had turned it all around.

The "M" word had entered his mind about five miles back, when he'd been wondering how he was going to return to his secluded cabin and live without her. Damn, but he wanted to marry her and the thought had his sweaty palms slipping on the steering wheel.

He checked his rearview mirrors again but no one had followed him out of DC and he wasn't too concerned. Whoever was looking for Hope would be at her house, lying in wait.

Going by the directions Hope had written down, he turned onto a side street and slowed. Her home was a tidy, two-story condo in a long line of identical condos. John made note of it but quickly scanned the surrounding area.

Sure enough, a boxy SUV was parked a few houses away on the opposite side of the street. As John cruised past, the man in the driver's seat didn't bother to look up from the map he was studying, but John noted his rearview mirror was cocked at an angle so he had a good view of Hope's front door.

After turning off the street, John made his way down another one, parked and got out. It was that time of morning when everyone had already left for work and those who stayed home were still inside eating breakfast and watching the morning news. John slipped between two houses and made his way to Hope's back door. Luck was on his side. There were no fences for him to vault and no curious dogs.

Hope's backyard was small and she'd packed a lot into the space. Flowerbeds lay fallow in the winter sun but he could picture what they would look like in the height of summer. Unfortunately, the trees and flowering shrubs were bare, leaving him exposed. He ran in a crouch to the house where he pressed his back against the wall. Senses attuned, his gaze skipped over the surrounding yards looking for anything out of the ordinary. Like Peruvians running toward him with guns. But of course it wasn't that easy.

After several minutes, he moved toward the back door, senses still open, gaze never resting. He easily picked the lock, shaking his head at her absolute lack of security. Any juvenile could get in. He stepped into the kitchen, pausing in the shadows, once again listening. Hope's home had the feel of abandonment but he still didn't move, learning long ago to never take anything for granted.

Eventually he moved through the house, checking each room thoroughly. This was the only time he wished Hope was with him because she would be able to tell him if anything had been disturbed. The place didn't look as if it'd been tossed, but he had no idea.

She'd converted one of her bedrooms into an office. Papers were scattered across her desk but it looked like the normal chaos of a cluttered desk. The other bedroom was in disarray, the furniture pushed to the middle of the room and covered with drop cloths. Half the walls were painted a pale green, the other half beige and dotted with putty. He wondered if this was the baby's room in progress. Her bedroom was clean, decorated in various shades of blue. No frills. He liked it.

On his way to the kitchen, he stopped in the living room and parted the front curtain with his finger to peer outside. The car was still there, the driver slumped in his seat. Idiot. If he didn't move, some nosy neighbor would eventually get curious and call the cops. Which would only help John's cause.

Pulling his cellphone from his pocket, he decided he could be a nosy neighbor.

After reporting the suspicious car, John searched the freezer. He had to push aside a gallon of chocolate-chip ice cream and a pound of hamburger before he found a zippered bag filled with frozen water. Suspended in the middle was the key.

By the time he was finished, a deputy was pulling up behind the car. John smiled and left the house through the back door just as his phone vibrated with a call from Luke.

"What's up, Barone?"

"Where are you?"

John heard the whine of an airplane engine in the background and the hairs on the back of his neck stood on end. "What's wrong?"

"We need to talk."

"So talk."

Luke pulled in a breath. "I just got word that Manco Garcia entered the United States two weeks ago."

John clutched the phone tighter. "How in the hell did a known terrorist get past airport security?"

"It appears Garcia used a fake name and disguised himself," Luke said.

He heard Luke talking about safety measures and what they thought had happened, but John's mind was on Hope. Hope who was alone.

It all made sense now—how Suzanne escaped, who had killed Charles Stewart. *Not Garcia. Anyone but Garcia.*

He sprinted across the backyards, having at some point closed his phone and tucked it into his pocket, not knowing if he'd ended his conversation with Luke. Pain shot up his leg, but thankfully it didn't buckle. When he reached his truck, he threw the frozen key on the passenger seat and revved the engine as he started it. Tamping down on the urge to race back to DC, he forced himself to drive slow, passed the man in the SUV and the deputy speaking to him.

John pulled onto the highway, his thumb poised over the numbers on his phone to call Hope when the phone vibrated again.

"Talk to me," Luke said after he answered. "What's going on?"

"I think Garcia came to the US to help Suzanne escape."

"How do you know this?"

John took a deep breath to collect his thoughts. Panicking wouldn't help Hope. "A few days ago a woman crashed into my front yard. Her name's Hope Stewart. Her father's Charles Stewart. Charles sent Hope to me for protection." John told Luke about the offshore accounts, about Charles' murder and the letter he left for Hope. "I have the key but I left Hope alone at your house." He dragged in a painful breath and stomped on the accelerator.

"Where are you now?" Luke asked.

"About thirty minutes away."

"Does she have the alarm on?"

"Yes."

"Good. If the alarm's tripped, it automatically goes to the DC police. They'll respond. My plane lands in ten minutes. Everything will be okay, John."

No it wouldn't. He had a terrifying feeling that nothing would ever be okay again.

"*Hope.*" John tore through the living room and into the

kitchen, Luke hot on his heels, yelling at the police who had pulled up at the same time. The back door was open, cold December air blowing through. He glanced around, taking in the clean kitchen and stepped closer to the running dishwasher to read the lit buttons as Luke walked in. "It's on the final rinse," he said.

"They can't have been gone long. Forty-five minutes tops."

John nodded. There'd been no sign of a struggle. That meant Garcia had surprised her, overpowered her immediately. Given the chance, Hope would have fought back. The fact she didn't was ominous.

"You think it was just Garcia? Or did he bring someone with him?" John asked. Luke hesitated and John pinned him with a glare. "What aren't you telling me?"

"When I saw Garcia had entered the country, I checked further," Luke said. "Seems Tómas and Ramon came through as well."

John stepped forward until he was toe-to-toe with Luke. "What the hell kind of screwed-up operation do you run if known terrorists can just waltz into our country?" Tómas and Ramon. They were ruthless, soulless. They wouldn't care that Hope was pregnant or that she'd known nothing about the money.

"Airport security doesn't fall under my jurisdiction, Callahan. I'm just reporting what I know. How they got in isn't important right now."

They stared at each other until John stepped back. "So the trinity's here."

"You need to calm down." Luke's voice was low, controlled and commanding, and it set John's teeth on edge.

"Yeah? I'll tell you that when it's Kate they have and watch you remain calm."

A speculative gleam entered Luke's eyes. "So it's like that, huh?"

John looked away, completely ill equipped to handle his emotions right now. "She's five months pregnant."

"What?"

"She's *pregnant.*"

Luke cursed.

"Exactly. So don't stand there and tell me to calm down."

"Maybe that will work to her advantage," Luke said. "Maybe because she's pregnant Garcia will—"

John laughed, the sound bitter and a tad on the wild side. "He killed his niece, Barone. Look what he did to us. What makes you think he'll spare Hope and the baby?"

Luke's lips thinned.

"You see now why we have to find her?"

"Where are you going to look?" Luke asked. "You have any idea where they took her?"

"None."

"You can't go running off half-cocked. We need to come up with some plan."

Luke was right, of course. But sitting and discussing this while Garcia had Hope made John's skin crawl.

"I think you'll hear from him soon," Luke said. "You have the key to the paperwork. Hope is the only one who can get inside that safety-deposit box. He'll call. And when he does, we need to be ready."

Chapter Sixteen

Hope's head hurt. She couldn't feel her arms or her legs. She had experienced panic and fear after waking up at John's with no memory, but that was nothing compared to this panic.

She was in a hotel room. A cheap hotel room. The carpet was threadbare, the comforter on the bed old and worn. The place smelled of mildew and rotten food and she had to force herself not to throw up.

"You're awake."

Her gaze flew to the corner of the room where the outline of a man stood among the shadows.

"What did you do to me?" Fear made her voice quiver. Her hand automatically tried to cover her stomach but she found they were tied. "What'd you give me?"

Garcia stepped into the light. "Relax, *querida.* It was nothing deadly."

She snarled and pulled at her bindings. Her wrists chafed against the rough rope as it dug into her skin. She tried to work her fingers around the knot.

"Save your energy, *querida.*"

She flung curses at him as she continued to struggle.

"Ah, now that is not nice." He chuckled, clearly amused.

Movement from the other bed caught her attention. A

woman leaned against the headboard and stared listlessly at Hope. She looked vaguely familiar. She had dark bags under her eyes, a nasty-looking bruise on her jaw and a puckered scar on her left cheek. Her clothes were cheap and nondescript, a white T-shirt and what looked like new jeans. Dull blonde hair was matted on one side and sticking up on the other. Who was she? She appeared to be drugged and Hope dismissed her as she continued to work on her bindings.

Garcia approached, a wicked gleam in his eye. "You can not escape," he said. "I will not allow it."

"Go to hell."

Anger flashed in the dark depths of his eyes and he leaned forward, invading her personal space. He smelled good. Like something exotic and masculine. The contrast of the evil coming off him and the deep scent of his expensive cologne was disconcerting. "I am going to hell, *querida*." He shrugged. "Just a part of doing business."

"What do you want from me?"

He straightened and pushed his hands into his pants pockets as he rocked back on his heels, staring at her through half-closed lids. "I want the money Susanita owes me."

"I don't know anything about any money."

His smile was malicious and she could have sworn she saw anticipation as well, which made her shudder. "It will be like that, eh?"

"I-I don't know about any money she owes you."

"Ah, but you know where it is, yes?"

She hesitated. She could hold out, not tell him. And he would beat her. John had barely survived this man's wrath, she surely wouldn't. And she had her baby to think of. "Yes, I know where it is."

Disappointment flashed across his face. Had he wanted her to hold out? To force the confession from her?

The woman slid off the bed and walked to Hope, hatred twisting her scarred features. “I want my money,” she snarled. “You had no right to it.” She reached out. Hope winced, fully expecting the woman to slap her but Garcia caught her wrist before it made contact.

“Not yet, Susanita.” Garcia pushed Suzanne back. “We have uses for Miss Stewart.”

This was Suzanne Carmichael? This dirty, unkept woman was the one who would have been First Lady? Who had ruined her father’s career, then killed him? Who had betrayed John and Luke and left them in a Peruvian prison? Hope curled her lip in disgust and hatred.

“Tell us where is my money.” Garcia’s smooth voice went hard.

€

John sat in his truck and stared at Daniel Webster’s dark house. It’d been five hours since Hope had gone missing and Garcia had yet to call.

He climbed out of the truck and headed toward the steps. The Christmas lights weren’t on and no lights shown from inside. With each step closer to the house, the sinking feeling in his stomach worsened.

He knocked, not really expecting an answer. Somehow Garcia had discovered Webster was friends with Hope. More than likely he’d gone through her house, found her mail, Christmas cards, address book. Anything that would lead him to her friends.

John cupped his hands and peered through the front window but couldn't see anything so he turned and headed back down the stairs. Webster loved Hope. John had seen it in the way the man's gaze tracked her every move, studied her face. He wouldn't have given her up without a fight.

Hands shoved deep into his pockets, John headed back to his truck.

"You looking for Daniel?" An older woman, wrapped in an oversized sweater, with house slippers on her feet, stood on the sidewalk across the street.

"You seen him around?" he asked.

"Ambulance took him away early this morning."

"Ambulance?"

The woman nodded. "Police say it was a burglary. Daniel got beat bad."

It was what he'd expected, but hearing the words made his stomach curl. Damn Manco Garcia. "I'm visiting from out of town. We were supposed to go out to dinner. Is he... Is he okay?"

She shrugged. "They say he might not make it." She tapped her head with a finger. "Damage to the brain, maybe."

Inside his pants pockets, his fingers curled into fists of frustration. "You know what hospital?"

"Georgetown University."

His hands were shaking as he headed for Luke's place. He had a damn good idea what happened. Somehow, Garcia discovered the connection between Webster and Hope. Webster had no doubt held off as long as he could, but in the end, he'd been no match for Garcia and had more than likely been the one to tell Garcia where Hope was. Having spilled many of his own secrets at Garcia's hands, John couldn't blame the guy. He just wished like hell he would have seen this coming.

"Did you hear anything?" Kate asked as John stepped inside the townhouse and shrugged out of his jacket. She'd flown to DC with Luke but Luke had kept her away from the house until he'd determined it was safe. Now John couldn't help but think *she* was *his* keeper, watching over him to make sure he didn't do anything stupid.

"Nothing."

She took his coat and hung it up. "I made coffee," was all she said before heading for the kitchen.

John dropped onto the couch and leaned forward, elbows on knees. He needed to pull it together, but all he could think of was Hope in the clutches of Garcia and Angelina's body lying in his cell.

"Drink this." A steaming mug was shoved under his nose and he automatically grabbed it.

Kate settled into a chair opposite him, curling her legs up underneath her. Dried paint freckled her fingers and colored her nails. She'd probably been painting while waiting for him.

John sipped his coffee. He'd met Kate on Luke's houseboat. The media had said Luke was dead, killed by his enraged ex-lover, Kate McAuley. John hadn't believed it at first, until Kate had arrived and admitted to it. She'd held her hands out and all but commanded John to arrest her.

John had liked her immediately.

"Tell me about Hope," she said into the silence.

He studied the dark liquid in his mug, the taste bitter on his tongue. "The smell of coffee makes her sick." He set the mug down. "I love her." He was surprised he'd spoken the words but not surprised at the feeling inside him. He'd known since last night he loved her, but he'd been too afraid to say it. Now he cursed himself for not telling her. What if she never knew? What if she died without knowing how he felt?

He shut his mind to that thought, absolutely refusing to believe he'd lose her after just finding her. "I never thought I'd find someone to love. Not after Peru." He rubbed his eyes with his fingers. "She's the only one who's been able to stop the nightmares, you know?" He paused to get his emotions under control. "If Garcia..."

"Luke says she drove all the way to Tennessee to find you."

He nodded.

"Seems to me that would take some strength of character. Don't count her out yet, John. She's a survivor, just like you."

He shook his head. "You don't understand. You don't know Garcia."

"I understand." There was a wealth of meaning behind those words. Of course, Luke would have told her. Suzanne's deception had torn Luke and Kate apart. They'd had a lot to work through to get to where they were today, but that didn't mean Kate understood. Not really.

No one could unless they'd lived through it.

Angelina's face came to mind. Not the smiling face that had delivered his meals, but the terror-filled face of someone who'd seen her own death. He bent his head and wiped at his eyes just as his phone rang.

John's and Kate's gazes collided before John lunged for the cellphone and thumbed it open. "Callahan."

"I want the key."

Kate leaned forward, her body tense as she tried to press her head to his to listen. Luke walked in and sat in the opposite chair, body calm but eyes sharp and clear.

"Yeah, well we can't always get what we want." John quoted the famous Rolling Stones song and Kate smiled, giving him a thumbs-up.

"You take me for a fool," Garcia spat. The heavy South American accent turned John's stomach.

"What do you propose, Garcia?"

"Give me the key or I hurt the pretty little *señorita*."

Hope was Garcia's ace in the hole, the only one left alive to get Garcia the money. He wouldn't kill the golden goose. Not until she handed over the documents needed to access the offshore account. So while intellectually John didn't believe Garcia would hurt her, emotionally the thought tore him apart.

"How about a trade-off," John proposed. "The key for Suzanne Carmichael."

Silence fell heavy between them. John's gaze went first to Kate, whose expression was sympathetic, then to Luke who nodded in approval. Against John's strenuous objections, they'd agreed to this plan. Luke had rationally countered every one of John's arguments until John had reluctantly agreed. With one provision.

"I want her away from Garcia before anything goes down," he'd told Luke. "I don't want Hope near any of that."

Luke had agreed.

"Look," John said to Garcia. "The woman doesn't mean shit to me. It's a win-win situation for you. You walk away with the girl and the money. I get Suzanne and some revenge."

Garcia chuckled and the sound, at one time so familiar, sent chills up John's spine. "You surprise me, *amigo*."

Yeah, well, that had been the plan. John's only surprise was that he could carry it off without falling apart.

"I never thought you were the type for revenge," Garcia

said. "But I wonder..."

There was a pause and John girded himself for what was to come.

"I am looking at her now." Garcia's voice went soft, almost musical. "I am looking at her hands bound behind her back, her legs spread before me, the look of terror in those beautiful eyes. Ah, *amigo*, it is *muy bonita*."

John clenched his jaw and bit back the possessive growl that strangled his throat. He could practically feel Hope's terror and the weight of responsibility lay heavy on his shoulders.

"Tell me, *amigo*, will she scream when I cut her? Or will she cry? Maybe she will beg for my mercy, eh?"

John nearly gagged. He didn't realize until Kate's hand came down on his back in a soothing gesture that he'd bent over, holding his stomach, breathing through his mouth. Garcia had always been a master at mental manipulation and he was honing his craft on John's mind. Probing, trying to determine if John was taking him for a fool. John had expected it, but nothing could have prepared him for it. His saving grace was that he and Luke had no intention of leaving Hope with Garcia long enough to find out.

But he wondered if the damage had already been done. In saving Hope's life, had he killed the best thing that had ever happened to him? Would she believe he would so readily give her up for revenge? For the hundredth time since he discovered her missing, John cursed himself for not telling her he loved her.

"Well, *amigo*? Will she scream? Or cry?"

John closed his eyes against horrific visions of Hope combined with images of Angelina's dead body. He struggled to breathe, concentrating on Kate's hand on his back. Before Hope, he would have never allowed Kate's touch. Because of

Hope, he was a whole man. Almost whole. He needed to free her first.

"It makes no difference to me whether she screams or cries, Garcia. I just want Suzanne."

There was another long pause. John held his breath, his gaze going to Luke's.

"*Bien.* Suzanne Carmichael for the key."

John exhaled silently. "Meet me at the bank. Three o'clock. You, Ms. Stewart and Suzanne. Leave Tómas and Ramon behind. I see any hint of those two and I'm outta there."

Garcia wouldn't want to be saddled with two useless women and no money. He'd leave the goons behind.

Garcia agreed and they disconnected. John's hands shook. He felt like a traitor to Hope and what they'd had together.

"This will work," Luke said. "We'll get her out of this."

John stood, ignoring his best friend, hating himself.

"John, you know this is the only way—"

Kate put a hand on her husband's shoulder. "She'll understand, John."

His gaze locked with hers and he had the horribly selfish wish that it was Kate in Garcia's grasp instead of Hope. He walked away, headed to the room he and Hope had shared for the past two nights. He sat on the bed and inhaled her scent that lingered in the air and wrote his last will and testament. He didn't have much, just a cabin in the middle of nowhere and a lot of money stashed away that he'd never use. He left it all to Hope and her baby.

Just in case.

€

Hope sat in the backseat of Garcia's SUV and stared straight ahead. As the minutes ticked by, the tension and silence inside the vehicle increased. Garcia remained still, but the muscle in his jaw began to tick as he watched people enter and exit the bank.

Garcia had given her another shot of whatever he had injected her with before. This one wasn't as strong, just enough to make her woozy but not enough to make her pass out. Her vision kept fading, as if she were watching the world through a fishbowl. If she turned her head, it took a moment for her brain to follow, so she tried not to move too much.

Deep inside, there was a sense of urgency, as if she needed to do something, but thoughts slipped through her mind like sand through her fingers and she couldn't grasp what that something was. The backseat was roomy but her knees were beginning to ache from being folded up and she needed to walk around. On top of that, Garcia hadn't allowed her to go to the bathroom before they left and the baby, thankfully active, had decided to use her bladder as a pillow.

Suzanne hadn't said a word.

Garcia suddenly straightened. Hope's heart lurched when she spotted John striding down the street. She got a funny feeling in her stomach, like butterflies that had nothing to do with the baby. He walked past the vehicle without looking inside and she stifled the urge to pound her fist against the window and scream his name.

At exactly three o'clock, Garcia and Suzanne got out. Cold air blew in bringing with it the sound of passing cars and even a few birds that had stayed for the winter. It was a relief to unfold herself from the SUV but her nearly numb legs buckled and she had to lean against the vehicle to get the feeling back.

John met them in the parking lot. The scene was so surreal, people going about their business as a terrorist and escaped convict stood in a parking lot. Hope wanted to scream at them to help her, to take notice, but at the same time she felt as if she were floating above everything, watching with detachment.

When they stopped in front of John, her stomach pitched and the world tilted. Her knees went weak again and only Garcia's firm hold on her elbow kept her upright.

"You have the key?" Garcia asked.

John fished in his jeans pocket and pulled out the key, dangling it in front of Garcia, then snatching it back, closing his fingers around it.

"Give me what I want first," John said.

Garcia put his hand on Suzanne and pushed her forward. Stunned, Hope could only stare at John who refused to meet her gaze.

This wasn't right. This wasn't how it was supposed to go down. At least not how she thought it was supposed to go down. Was it? She wished her mind was working better because she had this strange feeling she should be doing something.

Suzanne gasped and shot Garcia a terrified look. "What are you doing?" she whispered.

Garcia shrugged. "The price of doing business, no?"

Suzanne's fingers dug into Garcia's arm. "You can't do this. That's *my* money."

Garcia yanked his arm away. "It is my money now, *querida*." His smile was evil, full of malice and something very close to glee. Hope shrank from him, her gaze going to John in a silent plea for help.

"What's it feel like to be sold out by someone you trust?"

John asked Suzanne as he dropped the key in Garcia's hand. "Nice doing business with you, *amigo*." He emphasized the amigo, drawing it out as if to mock him.

Suzanne squirmed in John's grasp. "Don't do this," she pleaded with Garcia. "Please, Manco. I'll give you more money. Whatever you want. Just don't do this."

John carted her off, leaving Hope with Garcia. Not once had he looked at her.

As Garcia led Hope through the bank doors, she stumbled blindly after him.

"What does it feel like to be his *puta*?" His breath brushed her neck as he chuckled. Hope tried to ignore him, tried to close her mind to Garcia's hideous suggestions. Her leaden heart thumped against her rib cage and she rubbed it with her free hand, wondering if she were having a heart attack.

They waited in line and Hope absently watched as a teller counted out bills to a woman while in the next line a young construction worker cashed his paycheck. Garcia shoved something into her hand and when she looked down, she saw it was her driver's license.

"What do you think John Callahan is doing to Ms. Carmichael, eh, *querida*?"

Hope turned her head away, refusing to allow him to goad her into saying anything. Her heart was heavy and it had nothing to do with the drugs. John's abandonment cut through the narcotics. A powerful antidote to their mind-numbing qualities. He'd said he would help her. He'd promised. So what now? Was she just supposed to hand over millions of dollars to a terrorist?

The construction worker finished his transaction, stuffed his money in his wallet and walked out whistling.

Once again Garcia leaned close and whispered. "Is he torturing her as I tortured him? Do you think she will scream as he did?"

Hope closed her eyes and felt a tear trickle down her cheek. No, she didn't believe it. Refused to believe John would abandon her for his own revenge. What was it he'd said? She struggled to remember. They had been discussing revenge and he'd said revenge was rarely worth the price.

The businessman in front of them signed a slip and flirted with the teller. In the background phones rang, people laughed.

Hope's head began to ache and she rubbed her temple. What would happen if she started screaming?

As if sensing her thoughts, Garcia tightened his hold on her elbow and they moved to the front of the line.

"May I help you?" the teller asked with a wide smile.

Hope opened her mouth but nothing came out.

Beside her, Garcia smiled at the woman, a polished smile that showed off his perfect teeth and flashing eyes. He oozed the essence of Latino lover and the woman blushed. "My fiancé would like to access her safety-deposit box," he said smoothly.

"Of course. Do you have the key?" She directed her question to Garcia who produced the key. "Meet me over there," she said, nodding to a half door with a latch on it.

Garcia steered Hope to the door. She stumbled over a crease in the rug but no one seemed to notice.

The teller ushered Hope through and Garcia started to step in as well.

"Are you Charles Stewart?" the teller asked.

The name of her father, coming from this woman's lips, startled Hope. Garcia hesitated, then shook his head.

"Then I'm afraid you'll have to wait out here. Only the

owners of the boxes are allowed in. I'm sorry." She sounded genuinely sorry as she took the key from him and Hope's ID from her.

The vault was small, filled with floor-to-ceiling metal doors on one side and two tiny rooms for privacy on the other. The air was stuffy and Hope found it hard to breathe. Yet being away from Garcia seemed to clear her mind a bit. "I need help," she whispered to the teller. "That man—"

"You're a lucky woman," the teller said as she put both keys in the box and turned them. "He's gorgeous. And that accent." She sighed as she pulled the box out and placed it on a table. She patted Hope's arm. "It will be all right," she said before leaving.

Hope lunged and caught the woman's sleeve. "Please. You have to listen to me—"

Suddenly an arm came around from behind her and snaked across her upper body as a hand covered her mouth, cutting off her words.

Chapter Seventeen

"Hope, it's Luke Barone," the voice said from behind her.

Hope stilled, her eyes going wide as she recognized the name of John's best friend. He quietly pulled her into one of the small rooms people used for privacy and stepped in front of her. "Are you all right? Did Garcia hurt you?"

She shook her head but the movement hurt. "H-he gave me something. Drugs."

Luke gently pushed her into a chair and squatted in front of her. His clear gray eyes searched her face. He was as tall as John but not nearly as bulky. Was dark compared to John's light. But even through the differences, Hope could see the resemblances. It was in the eyes. Luke Barone had looked at death and then beaten it, just as John had.

"We'll get you checked out as soon as possible," he said. "Meanwhile I need you to stay in here. Do not leave this room until I come for you." He paused as he studied her once more. "Do you understand me, Hope?"

She tried to nod but a sharp pain made her wince. Slowly the fog that had shrouded her thoughts began to lift, but as it did, it made her weak. "John?"

"He wanted to be here but he had to do the swap for Suzanne. Believe me, Hope, it took all my considerable powers of persuasion to keep him from you." She blinked and Luke cursed. "Hope, are you understanding any of this?"

"Yes." Her relief was enormous. Even though she hadn't wanted to believe John would leave her with Garcia, she hadn't been sure. Suzanne in his clutches had to be a powerful lure.

Luke straightened from his crouched position. "Stay here. Either John or I will come for you."

Outside the vault, voices rose as people scuffled about. Luke disappeared through the doorway. When Hope stood, the room spun and she had to brace her hand on the small table.

The voices quieted until there was only one left. Calm, steady, a voice Hope had come to love.

"It's over, Garcia. Put the gun down."

She made her way to the door and peered out. The tellers, the construction worker who she'd thought was cashing his check, the businessman who'd flirted with the teller, Luke and John, all had guns pointed at Garcia, who had an arm around the friendly teller's neck and a gun to her head. The woman's face was white with terror, her eyes darting around as her fingers clawed at Garcia's arm.

But Garcia wasn't looking at her. He was looking at John and something inside Hope pushed through the drugs, clearing the way for an anger such as she'd never felt before. Garcia's taunts and innuendos hadn't affected her as much as seeing him with John, smiling that cruel, sadistic smile that she knew lived in John's nightmares.

"I want my money and safe passage out of the country," Garcia said.

"We don't negotiate with terrorists," John shot back.

Hope looked behind her and spotted the long metal box that contained everything Garcia wanted. The money that had driven Suzanne to sell arms to the wicked. The money her father died for and John had suffered because of.

Ignoring the nausea churning in her stomach and knees that threatened to give out with each step, she grabbed the box by its handle and walked to the center of the bank. Luke tried to grab her as she passed but she sidestepped him. “Manco Garcia.”

Garcia spun around, dragging the terrified teller with him. Hope held up the safety-deposit box. “This what you’re looking for?”

“Hope, no.” John’s voice was low but the control was edged with panic.

“You want your money?” she taunted the terrorist.

Garcia’s gaze flicked between her and the box.

“Let the woman go. Take me.”

“For God’s sake, Hope.” John took a step forward but was stopped by the businessman.

“They won’t let you out of this bank alive, Garcia. Unless you have me with you.” She didn’t know who or what was putting the words in her head, but she was glad they were there. This was going to end. Today. She was tired of running. Tired of living in fear. Tired of it all.

“Shoot him,” someone yelled.

“*Hold your fire,*” John shouted back.

Hope and Garcia stared at each other. The people around her began to dim, the edges of her vision blurred and her head swam. “Let the woman go,” Hope said softly. “Take me.”

John made a sound somewhere between anguish and outrage. Hope curled her fingers tighter around the handle of the box. Garcia released the teller and she stumbled away, sobbing. One of the female agents grabbed her and they disappeared into an office.

Now there were just the two of them, alone in a circle of men and women with guns pointed at them. Curiously, Hope didn't feel afraid. Maybe because she was finally taking charge.

"Hand me the box, *querida*."

Hope shook her head and tried to hide the wince of pain. "If you want it, you have to come and get it."

He looked at the crowd, all federal agents, Hope assumed.

"Don't do this, Hope."

She glanced at John and could see the truth in his eyes. If the agents started shooting, she'd be caught in the crossfire.

Garcia stepped forward.

"It's your only way out alive." She willed him forward, sensing she didn't have much time. Her legs began to shake and cold sweat bathed her forehead and rolled down her back. The heaviness of the metal box kept her rooted in reality.

Garcia lifted his chin, pulling his arrogance around him like a shield. She could see he understood what was happening. If he didn't come to her, he'd be shot. Yet he knew she had some plan up her sleeve but couldn't figure out what.

She blinked to clear her vision and he was suddenly in front of her. His quick movement caught her off balance and she swayed.

A grin spread across his face and something inside her broke open. A fury she'd never felt before flowed through the ragged opening, filling her muscles with the strength of ten men.

With a cry of rage, she lifted the box and swung. Metal collided with skin and bone to make a sickening crack. Blood splattered and Garcia went down. As the agents swarmed around him, Hope stumbled back, the box falling from her fingers. She stared at her feet where papers had scattered. *The* papers.

Hands gripped her shoulders, held her steady. Slowly she lifted heavy lids. John looked at her, emotions she didn't have the energy to identify crossing his features.

"You deserve peace," she said before her knees buckled and she sank to the ground.

€

"How is she?"

On the other end of the line, Luke made a noise that sounded suspiciously like a snort. "Why don't you come over here and find out?"

John leaned his head back and closed his eyes. He felt pain everywhere, but most especially in his soul. "I don't want to play games, Barone."

"How do you think she is? She's about ready to fall apart. For some odd reason, she's been spending a lot of time with Kate's brother."

Eric McAuley, US Marshal. The "businessman" inside the bank. Eric and Hope had a lot in common. They'd both lost loved ones so it was natural they would gravitate toward each other. Didn't mean John had to like it. Didn't mean he'd do anything about it either.

"How's the baby?" he asked.

"The baby's still active and the vital signs are good."

He couldn't help his rush of relief. As soon as Hope and Garcia had walked up to him in the parking lot, he'd realized she'd been drugged. His anger had been tremendous and it'd taken all his willpower to go through with the plan when what he'd wanted to do was wrap his hands around Garcia's neck and squeeze the life out of him.

His blood had run cold when he saw her walk right into the middle of everything with guns pointed at her, that damn metal box clutched in her hands, eyes flashing a temper he'd never known she possessed. And when she'd collapsed into his arms, he'd never felt such stark fear. After the fear came the anger. She'd been an idiot to put herself and her baby in danger. If he hadn't known he loved her before, he did then. And he could have seriously strangled her.

It'd been a brilliant move. Something he'd grudgingly admitted only after everything was over. But it was her last words that had made him run.

You deserve peace.

She'd done it for him. Risked everything so he could find peace. What she didn't know was that without her in his life, he'd never find that peace. And that's what made him run. The thought of needing her that much had scared him. Little did he realize the separation he'd forced between them was worse than the fear.

"The funeral for Charles Stewart is tomorrow," Luke said.

"Is it?"

"Damn it, Callahan. Snap out of this. She needs you."

John lifted his head and stared at the beige wall of the hotel room he'd rented three days ago. *She needs you.* He hadn't wanted to be needed a week ago. Hadn't wanted the responsibility that went with that emotion. Now he couldn't seem to get away from it. Because he needed her too.

But... It was complicated. Or maybe he was making it more complicated than it needed to be. He didn't know. He just knew he was afraid. Afraid to take that final step. "How'd you do it?" he asked Luke.

"Do what?"

For a moment he couldn't speak through the lump that suddenly formed in his throat. "Come back from the dead."

"Ah."

He didn't need to say more. Luke would know. Luke would understand.

"It hurt like hell," his friend admitted. "But Kate made it okay. Hope can do the same if you let her."

If he let her. That's where he always got tripped up.

"John."

"Yeah?"

"Go to Hope."

Go to Callahan. The words echoed in his mind. Her father had sent Hope to him for protection and in a bizarre twist of fate, she was the one who had saved him. He disconnected his call and stared at the wall.

Go to Hope.

It sounded so damn simple.

€

Hope stared at the churned ground, an ugly slash that reminded her of everything she'd lost. A cold wind blew but she didn't shiver, just pushed a few errant strands of hair out of her eyes as she stared at her father's grave.

The mourners had left. There hadn't been many since her father had lost so many friends because of the Carmichaels. There'd been more media than anything, but thankfully, Luke's men had kept them away.

The Barones had become her rock over the last four days

and she couldn't even begin to express her gratitude. Kate had stayed with her at the hospital through endless, terrifying tests to determine what Garcia had injected her with and if it harmed her baby. Thankfully, the baby was healthy.

She'd been introduced to Kate's brother, Eric. Ironically, it'd been Eric she'd gravitated to, recognizing the bleakness in his gaze, sensing he understood her loss. Only Eric would let her sit quietly, lost in her thoughts. Only he seemed to understand.

Manco Garcia sat in jail, awaiting trial. Suzanne Carmichael was back in prison. Thanks to Ramon and Tómas who had been picked up at the old hotel Garcia had used to keep Suzanne in, they'd found her father's body. Charles Stewart had been buried in a shallow grave in the woods behind his house. Luke and Kate wouldn't let her identify his body, opting to use dental records instead. She'd been grateful.

They'd helped with the funeral preparations, fielded calls from the media and sat with her during the endless police questioning, but when she'd asked about John, they became tight-lipped. Kate had seemed more sympathetic, Luke irritated. But the only thing either of them had been able to tell her was that John was busy being debriefed.

She'd believed it at first. But it'd been four days and she'd held out the irrational hope he'd show up at her father's funeral. Through her grief, she'd surreptitiously scanned the crowd, searching for his distinctive head of hair.

She bent and touched the cold ground. "I love you, Daddy." For the umpteenth time, tears filled her eyes and she dashed them away with the back of her hand. Whatever he'd done, he hadn't deserved this—brutal death, his body discarded. She missed him so much it was a constant ache inside her. John had said it would dim but sometimes she wondered.

She placed a single red rose on the heap of dirt.

A scarred, yet still-beautiful hand placed another next to it.

She looked up into guarded navy eyes. He reached down to help her stand, the feel of his hand on her elbow both comforting and heartbreaking.

"I'm sorry I missed the funeral," he said, standing awkwardly in front of her. He shifted, putting the bulk of his weight on his good leg. "I blew it, didn't I?" When she didn't answer, a pained look crossed his face.

The wind blew a piece of her hair across her mouth. John hooked it with a finger and gently tucked it behind her ear, his gaze following the movement. He shoved his hands into the pockets of his jacket and hunched his shoulders. "I'm sorry, Hope. It about killed me to walk away from you outside that bank. If there had been any other way, I would have taken it."

"I love you," she blurted out.

He froze, his gaze zeroing in on her. "What?"

"I love you." Hope held her breath. She didn't really expect a response. After all, John Callahan was a man who liked his solitude and she was definitely a woman in which very soon solitude would be a thing of the past. She took a step away. "Thank you for coming. And thank you for everything you've done. I know it wasn't what you had planned." She couldn't miss his wince. She hadn't meant to dredge all that up, just to express her gratitude. But it went far beyond gratitude. She and her child owed John their lives and no amount of words or gestures could express her appreciation.

"When you crashed into my life, I was desperate." He shrugged. "It's hard to explain. I don't even think I understand it all that well. I just know that after you, things changed. Everything wasn't dark and depressing anymore and I looked forward to waking up in the morning to see your face." He stared into her eyes. “I don’t want to go back to that. I don’t want to wake up feeling so alone it physically hurts.”

She licked dry lips. “Wh-what are you saying?”

He looked at her as the birds chirped in the trees and far off a car passed on the road below them. The cold January wind blew but she felt insulated from it. “I’m saying I want to live. I’m saying I love you.”

“There’s not just me to consider.”

He glanced at her belly, then placed his hand on top of it. The baby, still very active, gave a kick and John smiled a lopsided smile. “I know that. I don’t know what kind of dad I’ll be, but I’ll try my hardest.”

Her chin trembled and she placed her hand over his, feeling the scars, loving the man.

“I called my parents yesterday,” he said. “I told them about you. They’d like to meet you. I know... I know you don’t have any family left, but you’re more than welcome to share mine.”

A step in the right direction. She knew how hard it must have been for him to make that call.

“Yes,” she managed to say through her tears.

She held her arms out. John walked into them, gathering her close and burying his face in her hair. “Your father was right,” he whispered. “He who has Hope has everything.”

About the Author

To learn more about Sharon Cullen, please visit www.sharoncullen.net. Send an email to Sharon at Sharon@sharoncullen.net or subscribe to Sharon's newsletter at http://groups.yahoo.com/group/Sharon_Cullen.

The true threat lies within the heart...

Deception

© 2008 Sharon Cullen

Love on the Edge, Book 1.

Kate McAuley once thought Lucas Barone loved her, and returned that love for all she was worth—until the day he walked away without a word. Now eighteen months later she answers a knock on her door and finds Luke on her doorstep, broken, bleeding and unconscious. He brings with him all kind of emotions, and all kinds of questions. Where has he been? Why did he leave? And what's an accountant doing with wounds like these?

As a covert ops specialist with the U.S. government, Luke deceived, betrayed and conned so many people he couldn't keep them straight—except Kate. Their time together was magical, until the call came and he was forced to walk away. For four long years, memories of her have kept him alive and sane. Now, hunted by his own government, desperate and injured, Kate is the only one he can trust.

Kate's innocent phone call for help sets in motion an evil that reaches the highest echelons of political power. With accusations of murder and treason hanging over their heads, it'll take every ounce of Luke's training, intelligence—and Kate's trust—to keep them alive.

Warning: Deep emotion, edge of your seat suspense.

LaVergne, TN USA
22 September 2009
158627LV00001B/108/P

9 781605 043401